Pathki Nana

Amazing Indian Children series:

Naya Nuki: Shoshoni Girl Who Ran
Om-kas-toe: Blackfeet Twin Captures an
    Elkdog
Soun Tetoken: Nez Perce Boy Tames a
    Stallion
Kunu: Winnebago Boy Escapes
Pathki Nana: Kootenai Girl Solves a Mystery
Moho Wat: Sheepeater Boy Attempts a
    Rescue
Amee-nah: Zuni Boy Runs the Race of His Life
Doe Sia: Bannock Girl and the Handcart
    Pioneers
The Truth about Sacajawea

Pathki Nana

Kootenai Girl Solves a Mystery

Kenneth
Thomasma

Jack
Brouwer
Illustrator

Ken Thomasma 2003

Tenth printing, July 2002

Library of Congress Cataloging-in-Publication Data

Thomasma, Kenneth.

    Pathki Nana : Kootenai girl solves a mystery / Kenneth
Thomasma.

        p.   cm.

    Summary: Shy and lacking in self-confidence, eight-
year-old Pathki Nana faces a difficult task when, according
to Kootenai tribal custom, she must go alone into the
mountains to seek a personal guardian spirit.

    1. Kutenai Indians—Juvenile fiction. [1. Kutenai Indi-
ans—Fiction. 2. Indians of North America—Fiction. 3. Self-
confidence—Fiction.] I. Brouwer, Jack, ill. II. Title.

    PZ7.T3696Pat   1991
                                            [FIC]—dc20

                                                                    92-14432

    ISBN 1-880114-10-0 (Grandview Publishing Company)
    ISBN 1-880114-09-7 (Grandview Publishing Company: pbk.)

Printed in the United States of America by Cushing-Malloy, Inc.

Grandview Publishing Company 1-800-525-7344

Contents

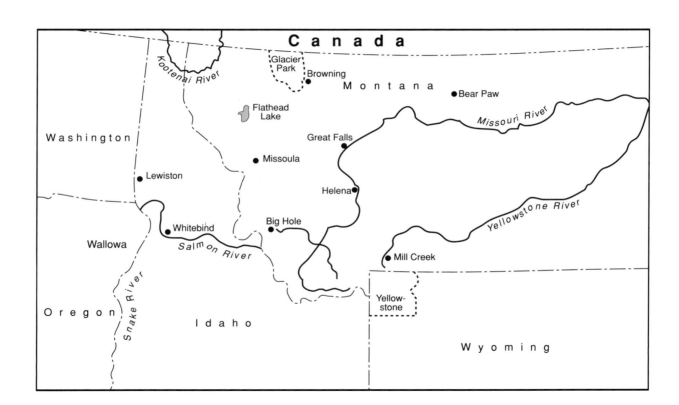

Appreciation Page

Phil and Karen Wilson of Kelly, Wyoming

Boys and girls of Star Valley, Wyoming

Metcalf, Holdaway, Afton, and Osmond Schools

Boys and girls of Kelly School, Kelly, Wyoming

Teton County Library, Jackson, Wyoming

Cameron Smart

Preface

The actual spelling of the name picked for the main character is Pa‡thki Nana. The Kootenai language has letters not found in our alphabet. The letter ‡ is one such. In the story this symbol has been omitted to make it easier to read. The girl's name is pronounced Päthkey Nänä. All the a's are pronounced as in "äh" or "fäther."

Research for this story was difficult. There seems to be no written study that the Kootenai people believe to be an accurate account of their culture and history. The people at the Salish-Kootenai College in Pablo, Montana, were very helpful. Sophie Matt of the Kootenai Cultural Committee was most gracious and knowledgeable. She helped me with her insight into the language and the nature of the Kootenai people.

The Kootenai Indians are a very proud people. They are very generous and soft-spoken and always stand willing to take in people in need. The generosity and kindness of these people has been well known for generations. They live in one of the most beautiful places in North America, the Flathead Lake area of northwest Montana. Theirs was not a buffalo culture. No large discoveries of gold were made in their lands. They had little competition for hunting and fishing grounds. As a result, the Kootenai people developed a unique society.

Pathki Nana was a part of the lower Kootenai bands. Upper Kootenai peoples lived farther north and into Canada. The modern Kootenai maintain their own unique identity while sharing a reservation with several other tribes headquartered in Pablo, Montana.

Pathki Nana: Kootenai Girl is historic fiction set in the 1780s. The horse was relatively new to all northwest Indian people at this time. The non-Indian had not yet appeared in any numbers.

1

Quiet One Speaks

Pathki Nana should have been a happy eight-year-old Kootenai Indian girl. Spring was her favorite time of year. The snow was melting away. Plants of every kind were springing to life. Soon good fishing would begin. There would be lots of fresh food. All around Pathki, children played in the warm sunshine. For these children it was a happy day.

Pathki Nana was anything but happy. The eight-year-old Kootenai girl walked alone, away from her village. Her head was down. Her eyes followed the path at her feet. Tears ran down her cheeks. Like many other times in her life, this young girl only wanted to be away from everyone.

Villagers were used to seeing "the sad one" go off to be by herself. No one could understand why Pathki acted this way. Even the girl herself could not explain her deep feelings. Ever since she could remember, Pathki seemed to do the wrong thing. It was as though some evil spirit led her into trouble over and over again.

On this day Pathki's mother had asked her to help get the noon meal ready. Pathki heated some rocks in the fire. She would put them into a hide container of water. The hot rocks would cause the water to boil. Strips of fresh fish meat would cook in the boiling water.

Pathki was anxious to surprise her mother by having the fish all cooked before her mother returned to their lodge. All went very well until the girl tried to remove the rocks from the hot water. She wasn't able to hold the hide container long enough, using just one hand. As Pathki tried to pull the first rock from the water, the container slipped from her hand. The water and the fish spilled onto the dirt.

At that exact moment the girl's mother came toward the fire. She was very upset to see the precious fish meat in the mud.

"Pathki, what happened? Why have you done this? Why didn't you wait for me to help you? You should know you can't do this alone! We do not have fish to waste!"

Pathki remained silent. Her head was down. She felt horrible. Her throat was choked. She couldn't say a word. Pathki dropped to her knees to pick up the strips of fish. Before she could start, her mother took her by the arm and pulled the girl to her feet.

"Pathki Nana, you have done enough here. Go now and gather firewood. That is something you are able to do. I will clean the fish. Go now!"

Pathki turned slowly and started around the side of their lodge. At the back of the shelter the girl came face to face with her sister. Red Willow was one year older than Pathki. The two girls got along fine most of the time, but Red Willow, like everyone else, did not understand why her sister seemed to be so unhappy so often.

The two sisters looked straight into each other's eyes for a few seconds. Then Pathki's head dropped. She kept looking down at the ground as she walked around her sister and away from their lodge.

"Pathki! What is it now? Why do you leave again?" shouted Red Willow.

"Red Willow, let her go," called the girls' mother. "She will return. I sent her for firewood. Come help me clean up the fish that your sister spilled."

Pathki walked faster and faster. Once again she had done the wrong thing. She did not blame her mother for being upset. Pathki knew she deserved to be sent away, only this time it was worse than ever. In her heart her plan was to please her mother by cooking the fish for her. It would have been a wonderful surprise. It would have been the first time she had done some cooking alone. She wanted her mother to be very proud of her.

Nine-year-old Red Willow had already cooked an entire meal for the family. Mother was so proud of Red Willow that she told everyone she met about the wonderful meal her daughter had prepared. Today Pathki couldn't even boil fish without ruining everything. The eight-year-old Kootenai Indian girl wondered if she would ever be able to do anything right.

As Pathki walked away, she paid very little attention to her surroundings. In no time she was deep into the forest. Suddenly she stopped. She looked in every direction as if she was lost. "Go gather firewood. That is something you are able to do." Her mother's words seemed to ring in Pathki's ears.

Slowly the girl began gathering dead branches from the forest floor. Her tears had dried on her cheeks. Pathki was alone with her thoughts. *Will I ever change? Will I ever be able to do things right? Will I ever be as good as Red Willow and the rest of the girls? Have I done something to make the Spirit angry with me? What have I done wrong?*

All these questions poured through Pathki's mind over and over again. Many times before she had asked herself these same questions. She was never able to find even one answer. Trouble seemed to follow her everywhere.

Carrying a large bundle of firewood, Pathki walked slowly toward her village. With her head down, the girl didn't see an old woman moving steadily toward her. Pathki's grandmother, Quiet One, walked just fast enough to meet her granddaughter at the edge of the village.

Quiet One was old and wrinkled. Her thin back was bent and curved. She could no longer stand up straight. Many years of living and hard work had worn Quiet One down. The sun and wind had weathered her skin. Pathki nearly ran into her grandmother before she saw her on the trail. For a few seconds the small girl and the weathered old one looked at each other in silence.

"Pathki, take the wood to your lodge. Return to me here at this place. I wish to have you hear my words. I want to help you." Without another word, the girl's grandmother turned off the trail and took a seat on a fallen tree.

Pathki paused to watch Quiet One sit down on the large log. The young girl was confused. *Why would the old one want to talk to me now?* Pathki wondered if she had done something else that was bad. The nervous girl began to worry about what Quiet One would say to her.

"Go, my child. Go with your wood. Come back to me. I have words you must hear." Quiet One's voice was very soft, as always. The way she spoke those few words made Pathki feel a little better. Somehow her fears of the worst possible thing happening were wiped away by her grandmother's calm voice.

Pathki quickly carried the firewood to her lodge. She avoided her mother and her sister as they prepared the noon meal. The spilled fish had been cleaned, and Red Willow was boiling them again. Pathki put her wood down quietly. Quickly she turned and walked back toward the forest.

The small girl had a strange feeling as she headed for the fallen tree where Quiet One waited for her. Pathki's heart beat faster and faster. Soon she would know why her grandmother wanted to talk to her. Somehow the girl knew something very important was about to happen to her.

The whole village knew that Quiet One had great wisdom. The people even believed that she had been given special powers by the Good Spirit. The old woman spoke only when she had something important to say. In a few minutes Quiet One would say words to Pathki that the young girl would carry in her heart the rest of her life. Pathki would never be the same after this spring day.

No one was around to see the small girl take a seat on the log next to her grandmother. At first Quiet One just smiled at Pathki. Then her smile left. The old one became very serious. She paused a few seconds before she began to speak. Pathki grew more nervous and anxious. She could barely sit still. Nothing like this had ever happened to her in her whole life.

"My child, again I see you are not happy. Many times I see you with your head down. Many times I watch you leave our village to be alone. Your life seems to be hard for you. I hope my words can help you."

Quiet One's words, spoken softly and steadily, made Pathki feel warm and calm inside. *Words to help me? How can words help me? What words does grandmother have for me?* The young girl had many questions but said nothing. Pathki fastened her eyes on Quiet One's wrinkled hands folded in her lap. The girl listened carefully.

"Pathki Nana, you are old enough now to know about your birth and your life. I was with your mother when you came out of her body. Your mother suffered much pain for a long time. Much blood came from her body. Even while she held you in her arms, we could not stop her bleeding. Your mother became weaker and weaker. She held you close to her body. Her face showed her great love for you. You were her firstborn. Your mother's joy was great, but she became weaker and weaker. We could not stop her bleeding. She lived only one day and one night. Oh! How we tried to help her. It was no use. The Spirit removed her to the spirit land. Just before she took her last breath, she asked us to love you and to care for you for her.

"Pathki, your mother did not give you a name. She used all her strength just holding you close. You have been called Pathki Nana, girl child, since your mother's death. I was the one who took you from your mother's arms. I gave you to Two Birds. She is your mother's sister. Red Willow is Two Birds' first child. Two Birds gave both of you her milk. She became your mother, too. Your birth father is Deer Runner. He lives in another village with his new family. He visits our village each summer."

Pathki felt lightheaded and dizzy. She could not focus her eyes. Quiet One's words poured into the small girl's mind like a great flood. *My mother died! She held me close! She suffered great pain! No one could save her! She asked that I be loved and cared for! I was given to Two Birds! She became my mother! Red Willow became my sister! My birth father is Deer Runner!*

Pathki was breathless. She felt like she was going to fall to the ground. She hardly noticed Quiet One move closer. The old one's arm came around Pathki. Her thin fingers gently squeezed the girl's upper arm.

"My child, your mother was my daughter. Two Birds is my daughter. I am your grandmother. I love you very much. When you are sad, I am sad. Now, my child, you know about your birth and your life. Soon you will be old enough to seek your guardian spirit. I know you will be a good person. You will find joy in your life. You will have a family of your own to love and care for. Go, my child. Walk straight. Work hard. Take the bad things that happen to you and let them make you a wiser and better person. Come to me when you are sad and troubled. Together, our words will bring wisdom and give our hearts reason to sing.

"Now I go. I will be here for you until the Spirit takes me from this life. Until then we will be here with each other."

Pathki watched in silence as Quiet One rose slowly. Her eyes followed her grandmother's progress until she was out of sight. Then the young girl sat looking at her own hands. She stared down at her bare feet. It was as if she was looking at a different person. For the first time ever, Pathki knew who she really was. This day would change her life. The girl would hold Quiet One's words in her heart forever. Before Pathki became a grown woman, her grandmother's words would help her greatly. They would help her survive great danger and even help her face death itself.

2

Forbidden Action

For a while Pathki's life appeared to get better. She seemed happier than she had ever been in her whole life. Maybe Quiet One's words had changed everything. A whole year passed with only a few bad days for nine-year-old Pathki. She even smiled more.

Quiet One took time to talk with her granddaughter often. She taught Pathki much about life and growing up. The girl had to spend many hours each day taking care of two younger brothers. She also helped pick berries,

23

dig roots, dry deer meat, and make pemmican. Best of all, Pathki liked preparing meals.

The first time Pathki made a whole meal by herself, it was the greatest day of her life. Two Birds told her she had done very well. The young girl felt good all over. She even became lightheaded. She walked more quickly than ever and felt an extra surge of energy. She thought she could do anything now.

How happy Pathki was that day! The very next day all of her happiness was wiped away. It all happened in an instant. Pathki never expected that what she tried to do would end up so terribly.

The early summer afternoon was a beautiful one. Young children had time to play. Pathki watched her two small brothers playing with friends in an open field next to the village. The boys, age three through five, were playing their favorite game. With their small bows and arrows the boys tried to shoot an arrow through a rolling hoop. The hoop was made from a green willow branch. This hoop was rolled past the boys. The boy who could shoot the most arrows through the rolling hoop was the winner. The hoop was rolled many times.

At first it was rolled close to the shooters. Then the hoop was rolled a little farther from the boys, making the shots harder and harder.

All the boys were extremely excited. They cheered each other loudly. Even the smallest boy could shoot some arrows through the rolling hoop. This game would prepare the boys to be expert hunters when they became young men.

Pathki watched the boys closely. She noticed that her five-year-old brother was holding his arrow to the bowstring differently than the other boys did. Pathki thought he was missing many shots because of the way his fingers held the arrow to the bowstring. Without thinking, Pathki walked up to her brother, took his bow from him, and showed him his mistake. The girl had never held a bowstring or even a bow before this time. As she held the arrow the way the best shooters did and pulled it back on the string, Pathki's fingers slipped. The arrow flew to one side, striking a four-year-old boy in the foot. The boy screamed and rolled onto the ground. The boy cried out in pain as he held his injured foot.

Pathki was stunned. She dashed to the sobbing boy. She raised him to a sitting position and blurted out words of comfort. The boy lurched away from the terrified girl. He jumped to his feet and limped off toward the village.

"Pathki! You have done a bad thing!" It was Red Willow. Pathki's sister had come up just in time to witness the accident.

"You know girls are never allowed to touch a bow and arrow. You have done it. You have hurt that boy. Why did you do it?"

Red Willow's words cut into Pathki like a knife. Her words stung like they were on fire. Pathki knew she was wrong. No one would care when she would tell them she was only trying to help her brother. Girls were taught from the beginning that they are never allowed to touch a bow and arrow, a spear, or any other weapon. Only boys and men were allowed to do this.

The first man to come out of the village to see what had happened was Cut Ears. He was the man that Pathki feared most. He was not a Kootenai Indian. He had come from a tribe on the eastern side of the great mountains.

Cut Ears came to the Kootenai village as a young man. He told about being driven from his own village unfairly. He said he had been accused of running away during a battle and letting his friends die. He said he was punished by having the tops of his ears cut off.

The Kootenai people had taken in this unfortunate man and allowed him to stay. Cut Ears was a tall and powerful man. His arms and legs bulged with muscles. Now he stood over Pathki with an angry look covering his face. His eyes seemed to look right through the trembling girl.

Immediately Cut Ears began shouting something in his own language. He waved his arms wildly. Pathki stood motionless with her head and shoulders down. Others came rushing from the village to investigate all the commotion. Instantly Cut Ears switched to the Kootenai language.

"This girl is evil! She takes up the bow and injures a boy! She does not know who she is! She is old enough to know weapons are not for girls!"

Cut Ears was interrupted by Two Birds. "Pathki, come with me!"

With a turn of her head, Pathki looked into her mother's eyes. Two Birds had a disappointed look on her face. She reached down and took Pathki by the upper arm. Two Birds guided Pathki past all the people who had come to see what had happened.

It seemed to Pathki that the whole world was looking at her. She felt horrible. How could a thing like this have happened? Just the day before she was the happiest she had ever been in her life. Now the worst thing possible had happened to her.

Two Birds led Pathki to their lodge. When inside, the girl's mother sat her down. Two Birds spoke in a calm but firm voice. She spoke for a long time. Over and over she told Pathki that she needed to use her head and act like other girls her age. She told her that if she was a boy she would be spanked.

When Two Birds had finished and left the lodge, Pathki just sat motionless. Now she never wanted to leave the lodge. She did not want to look at anyone or let anyone see her. Pathki just stared at the ground between her feet. It seemed as if hours had passed. The girl felt ashamed, worthless, and miserable.

When her father returned from hunting, he entered the lodge. For a long time he lectured Pathki about never touching a weapon again. He told her over and over that weapons were for boys and men, not girls. He said all girls need to spend their time doing only things that would prepare them to be good wives and mothers.

After her father finished, Pathki felt a little better. At least all the words had been said. Now she would be left alone. Now the unhappy girl could begin to forget this awful day.

But Pathki could not forget. That night she could hardly get to sleep. When she did sleep, she had terrible dreams. Every dream ended with people shouting at her and telling her to act like every other girl in the village. Pathki rolled and tossed all night.

Before the sun came over the eastern mountains, Pathki was up. She walked in the early morning light to the river that was close to the village. Walking upstream on the riverbank, the girl came to a little-used trail, which led uphill into the forest. The mountain trail was very narrow. In places Pathki had to step over fallen trees that lay across the trail. The morning was still and quiet.

Pathki was startled by a grouse that suddenly flew up in front of her. The frightened girl began to shake. At the same time a squirrel broke out into a loud chattering. He was telling Pathki she was too close.

The girl moved on at a steady pace. Even she had no idea when she would stop. Coming to a fork in the trail, Pathki turned right. Here the trail climbed steeply through the dense pine forest. On and on the girl climbed. She thought of what it would be like to just keep going and never come back to her village. Maybe she could find a new place to live.

While many confusing thoughts flooded Pathki's mind, she came to a place in the trail where she suddenly found herself in the open. For the first time in hours, she stopped. She had lost all track of time. Her eyes searched the treeless mountainside above her. She focused on a high rocky ledge at the summit.

Without hesitating, Pathki started upward. She hiked faster and faster, straight for the high rocks. It was almost as if she knew that the rock slab would have a great secret to show her.

Pathki was out of breath. She was gasping for every breath as she neared the base of the steep cliff. She found a rock-strewn gully that led to the top. Carefully Pathki scrambled up the depression in the wall. The last ten feet was vertical rock, but there were plenty of good foot- and hand-holds to help her climb the wall. At the top she scraped all the loose debris away. Then she raised her right leg to the top and rolled herself over onto the summit slab.

Pathki rose to her feet. The rock felt smooth to her small bare feet. She weighed only sixty pounds. Her deerhide dress hung loosely from her thin shoulders. A slight breeze blew through her long black hair. Her dark brown eyes sparkled in the bright sunlight.

As she looked out over the spectacular mountain valleys, Pathki almost forgot her troubles. She could see for miles and miles in every direction. Mountains and valleys stretched out to the horizon everywhere she looked. The tiny girl stood in one place for a long time. She only moved enough to look east, west, north, and

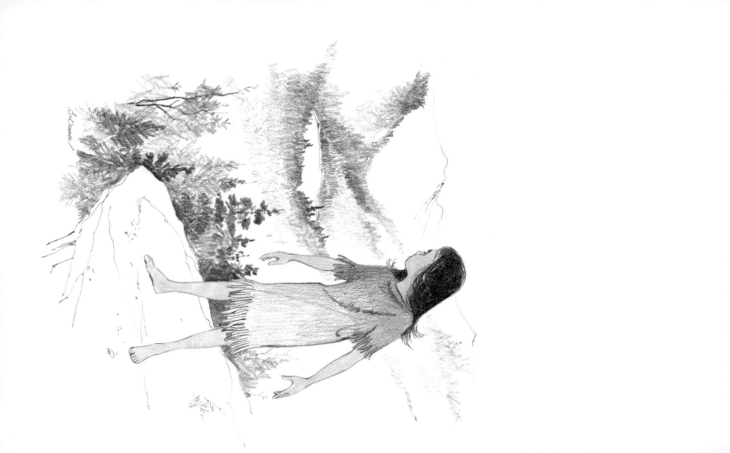

south. Her dark eyes studied every mountain and every valley. She could see several high mountain lakes. To the west a distant waterfall looked like a silver thread hanging between the trees.

Pathki's eyes passed over the vast scene several times. She kept coming back around to look at one special lake far to the north. For some strange reason she was attracted by this deep blue lake. It sparkled like a giant sapphire suspended in the high valley. Pathki had no way of knowing that this lake, now so far away, would someday become one of the most important places on earth to her.

All day long Pathki had walked along as if she was in another world. Time had meant nothing to her. Suddenly she was startled back to her senses. Her eyes turned west to the sun. It was on its way down. The day would end soon. Instantly she realized she couldn't make it home before dark. Now what could she do? Would her mother be angry? Was she in even more trouble? Had she made another bad mistake? Where could she spend the night? Would a grizzly bear or mountain lion be waiting for her on the trail back?

Pathki spun around and carefully climbed down the wall to the gully. She slipped and slid through the gully to the grass. Pathki skidded and stumbled through the grass on the open mountainside. When she reached the trail, it looked like an old friend. She was on her way home. Now she could think more clearly.

Pathki began to form a plan. A safe shelter would be absolutely necessary. At first light in the morning, she would head for home as fast as possible. Then what? *What will I say to my mother? What can I do? I must think of something.* The girl became more and more upset. She didn't have any answers. She was beside herself.

Pathki walked on in deep thought. Suddenly a strange feeling came over the frantic girl. It happened in a mystical way. It seemed to Pathki that a voice was coming to her. It was Quiet One's voice as clear as ever: "Come to me when you are sad and troubled. Our words will bring wisdom and give our hearts reason to sing."

Then Pathki spoke aloud. "Quiet One, I'm coming. I need you. Please be there to help me."

3

Evil Awaits

Now Pathki had her answer. When she reached her village, she would go right to Quiet One. She could tell her everything. *Grandmother loves me. She will have the wisdom I need,* thought Pathki. These thoughts gave the girl much comfort.

Soon the trail was in deep shadows. In a short time it would be dark and unsafe to go on. Pathki had heard stories of children and even adults walking right up to grizzly bears in the darkness. Most of these people were never seen again. The bears would carry them off and devour them.

As darkness closed in on her, Pathki came to a low overhanging boulder. Moss and lichen covered this huge rock. It was like a giant shelf hanging above the ground. On her knees the girl could crawl back under the slab for fifteen feet. It made a perfect roof for a shelter.

This was the place Pathki needed. The three-foot-high space would be her shelter for the night. As far back as she could crawl, Pathki quickly leveled a place for her bed. Next she squirmed out of her shelter to gather large clumps of moss for a mattress. She followed this with the addition of large logs. She rolled them under the overhang to use for a wall in front of her bed. Pathki used large rocks to hold the logs in place.

Just as darkness made it impossible to see, Pathki had completed the last work on her shelter. She wiggled her way through the narrow opening she had left for a door. As she stretched out on the soft moss, Pathki's stomach began making strange noises. She had walked all day without food. She had made only two stops to take drinks from small streams. It was like the day had been a dream. She wouldn't sleep much. Every sound would bring her wide awake.

In the middle of the long night, Pathki woke up. She could hear the sound of loud breathing. A large animal was standing right next to the overhang. It was less than fifteen feet from Pathki. The frightened girl knew she must lie absolutely still. This animal did not know it was a girl under the rock. Neither did the beast know if she had a weapon. The less the animal knew, the better it would be for this petrified girl.

After what seemed like an hour, the animal left. Pathki stayed awake for a long time, waiting for the animal's return. Once again her thoughts were on Quiet One. Oh! How Pathki needed her grandmother. Quiet One would have wise words for a confused girl child.

Pathki closed her eyes. She could see Quiet One's wrinkled face and her shriveled hands folded on her lap. Pathki could see Quiet One sitting next to her mother as she lay dying. Pathki could see Quiet One take a tiny baby from a dead mother's arms. She saw her hand the infant to Two Birds.

Pathki rolled and tossed in a fitful sleep as she dreamed and dreamed. The howl of a great grey wolf caused the girl to come wide awake. She raised up to peer over her log wall. It was still pitch dark, but Pathki knew daylight had to be near.

Pathki was stiff and sore. She shivered in the cold, damp air. Slowly she dragged herself out from under the overhang. When she stood up, she felt weak and dizzy. She had to lean against a giant fir tree. Soon she slumped to the ground. She dare not leave yet. It was still too dark. If she could have seen the ground right next to her, she would have spotted the paw print of a giant grizzly bear. He was the animal she had heard breathing, just fifteen feet from her bed that night.

Once again all the thoughts Pathki had since she left her village began to race through her mind. She was happy to see faint light in the sky above the dense trees. As soon as she started walking, Pathki felt better. A stop for a long drink of water helped her even more.

Pathki walked in the early morning light, going as fast as possible. Several times she stumbled over roots still hidden in the poor light. As the day brightened, the anxious girl walked even faster. Somehow she seemed to know that the sooner she reached her village, the better it would be for her. How could she know that this day would change her life forever!

The Kootenai village was next to a river in the northwest corner of the state we now call Montana. From a distance Pathki could hear dogs barking and children playing. People hardly noticed her walk by them. Women were busy with their never-ending tasks. Men were off hunting and fishing.

Pathki searched everywhere for Quiet One but couldn't find her. Coming around a group of lodges, the girl almost bumped into her mother.

"There you are! Take this water! I have been doing your work. Go straight to the lodge."

Two Birds' words caused Pathki to swallow hard and to feel as if every eye in the village was on her again. The unhappy girl followed her mother to their lodge. The two heavy skins full of water weren't even noticed by Pathki, who could only wonder what would happen to her back at the lodge.

Back home it didn't take Pathki long to find out what would happen. "Put the water in its place," Two Birds said, "You have much work to do. First you cause trouble. Then you run off and are gone all night. Pathki, it is time for you to leave the village and seek a guardian spirit for your life. Maybe there is a spirit that can lead you to a more responsible life. Maybe there's a spirit that can teach you to behave like other girls your age."

Every Kootenai girl knew that one day she would have to go to the mountains alone. Each girl would find a place to stay completely alone for days. There would be no eating, drinking, or sleeping. There a girl would receive a vision in which she would meet her guardian spirit. Often the spirit would appear in an animal form. This animal would have something great to teach the one it visited in the vision.

Two Birds' words rang in Pathki's mind: " . . . time to leave and seek your guardian spirit, time to leave, time to leave."

Yes, I will leave. I will seek my guardian spirit, thought Pathki. *I'll leave today!*

Instantly it seemed like a giant weight had been lifted from Pathki's thin shoulders. Maybe this was the answer to the unfortunate girl's problems. "I am a Kootenai girl! I'll go! I'll find my guardian spirit! This is the time! My whole life will change! Thank you, mother who loved me. You gave me life. Thank you, Quiet One, for your words and your love. Thank you, Two Birds, for sending me to seek my guardian spirit. Thank you for letting me be your daughter." Pathki wanted to shout these words out. Her body trembled with excitement. Today was her day. Today she would go.

Pathki kept busy at her usual tasks all morning. She helped prepare the noon meal. She had to force herself to keep her mind on her work. It wasn't easy. She kept thinking about her plan to leave.

"Today I leave," she told herself. "I must tell Quiet One. I must find her. I will leave and stay away for days. Quiet One will send me off with words of wisdom. I will find my guardian spirit. I will become a new person. I will have a new life."

At the same time these words were filling Pathki's mind, another person was making plans to leave the village. This person was leaving for a very different reason. Pathki and this man were headed for a meeting neither of them wanted to happen. Their meeting would trigger unbelievable terror in the small girl. She could not know what horror awaited her that very day.

Pathki ate the noon meal of deer pemmican, dried roots, and boiled fish. She sat off away from her family, deep in her thoughts. This would be her last meal for days. Pathki could hardly swallow. Her hands trembled with excitement that she had never experienced before. To leave the village and stay in the forest alone for days—this would make any boy or girl shake with excitement.

What would happen in the days ahead? Would she find a powerful guardian spirit? Would she come back as a new person? The answers to these questions would be more unbelievable than any girl could imagine.

Pathki already knew where she would go. She planned to follow the same trail she walked the day before. She planned to spend her first night in the overhanging shelter. The next day Pathki would climb back to the beautiful rock ledge. There she would stay as she waited for the vision of her guardian spirit. Pathki could not know that her plan had no chance of ever being carried out. No, something would happen to put Pathki in great danger even before she reached the overhanging rock.

Pathki finished eating. She helped put the leftover food in storage. After one quick trip to fill the waterskins, the tense girl headed for the edge of the village. No one paid any attention to her as she walked past the last lodge. Pathki was relieved to be headed away from all those who might say anything to her. She walked a little faster with each step she took.

Just when Pathki thought she was out of everyone's sight, she was shocked to see Quiet One waiting for her. Her grandmother was sitting on the same log where they had had their long talk. Without a word spoken, Pathki walked to her grandmother. The old one's eyes looked sad and thoughtful. As Pathki sat down, Quiet One began to speak. Her voice was even more soft and slow than before.

"My child, I know where you are going. I heard your mother's words. I will tell Two Birds you have left to seek your guardian spirit. Pathki Nana, you should have told

her yourself. Two Birds loves you, too. I know it is hard for you to speak about your feelings. This you must learn to do. Honest words are always good for everyone.

"Granddaughter, you do not have to speak to me. Keep your thoughts in your heart. Return to us when you are ready. Like your mother who gave you life, you, too, can have great love in your heart. When you come back to us, you will no longer be a girl. You will be a young woman. Go now, my child. Go with my love."

Pathki's eyes swelled with tears. Her throat choked with emotion. She threw her arms around the old one's neck. Quiet One cried softly as she returned Pathki's hug. After a few minutes the girl gently pulled away, stood up, and ran toward the trees. At the edge of the forest the girl stopped to watch Quiet One walk slowly toward the village. Grandmother looked more bent over and weaker than ever.

As soon as Quiet One disappeared into the village, Pathki headed up the familiar trail. In a short time she was far into the trees. At the fork in the trail, she turned right again. Pathki was very excited to be on her way to her great adventure.

Only a short distance from the fork in the trail, Pathki came to a sudden stop. She could not believe what she saw at her feet on the trail. She was alarmed to see fresh horse droppings. She asked herself, "What is a horse doing on this trail? There were no droppings here this morning. Will I see this horse ahead? Is there a rider with this horse? I do not want to meet anyone now."

Pathki was confused. She didn't know what to do. She wanted to get to her ledge but did not want to meet anyone on the way. Pathki looked both right and left. She decided to leave the trail. On the right she could travel through the trees just above the trail. She could keep the trail in sight most of the time without being seen very easily by anyone on the trail.

The Kootenai people had only had horses for about twenty years. They had only a few horses, using them mainly to carry deer, elk, moose, and bear meat after a hunt. Most of their travel was done by canoe on the many lakes and rivers.

There was no good reason for a horse to be on this trail. No hunters would be on this steep trail at this time of day. Maybe this horse had just wandered off from the village and was lost. Pathki thought she might be able to catch it and take it back to her village. This would be a great thing for her to do. This would make everyone say good things about her.

No, the horse leaving the fresh signs was not lost. No, it was not alone. No, Pathki would never go near this horse. To do so would cost Pathki her life. When she did see this horse, the girl would be witness to an event that would solve a puzzling mystery that had existed in her village for over a year. With every step she took, Pathki came closer and closer to a sight that would freeze her in her tracks.

Cut Ears' Betrayal

4

Fallen trees covered the forest floor. Pathki used her keen sense of balance to walk on the downed timber. The girl had always been good at crossing streams on logs lying across the water. She knew the importance of keeping her eyes focused on the log at a spot five or six feet in front of her feet. This keeps a person from losing balance. Pathki had great balance.

The girl traveled quietly and easily at an angle parallel with the trail. She kept herself hidden most of the time. In a short time Pathki's route was blocked by a dense growth of tangled bushes. The thick bushes grew in the damp soil of a drainage ditch. The tangled mass went all the way up the mountainside to a moss-covered rock cliff that dripped with moisture. The only way around the barrier was to Pathki's left. This would take her down closer to the trail, but she had no other choice.

Pathki came through the bushes at a place only ninety feet from the trail. She walked just thirty feet beyond the bushes and stopped. Instantly she dropped to the ground. Pathki spotted movement just below her. She couldn't see what it was. She didn't have to see it. The sound she heard told her the answer. A horse blew air from its nose and mouth. There was a horse on the trail only a short distance from the hidden girl!

Pathki didn't move a muscle. She had to think about what to do next. She needed to find out if the horse was alone. If it was, she would think of a way to catch it. If someone was with the horse, she would have to stay hidden. Pathki did not want to be seen by anyone.

The girl hugged the ground and started moving forward on her stomach. Ahead were two large fir trees growing very close together. Pathki planned to worm her way forward to them. There she could stand hidden by the trees. She would be able to look between them without being seen.

As the girl inched her way forward, the horse blew more air from its mouth and nostrils. Pathki's ears told her the horse hadn't moved. Why had the horse stopped? There was no grass to eat. Maybe water was crossing the trail there. The girl would find out soon.

Pathki finally squirmed up to the two giant fir trees. Slowly she pulled herself to her feet. She was careful to remain hidden behind the larger of the two trees. She took time to catch her breath. Now she was ready for a look.

Cautiously Pathki moved one eye past the large tree. What she saw shocked her. Fear and terror poured over the small girl. The horse was not alone! It was tied to a rope held by a large man. Pathki would have recognized this man anywhere. He was the last man she would ever want to meet out here. Standing right next to the nervous animal was Cut Ears. He had his back to the girl. She could see his deformed ears on each side of his long braid of hair.

Cut Ears! Why is he here? Why does he have one of our horses? He does not ride it. He is not carrying meat to our village. Why does he stop here where there is no grass or water? Why is he on such a steep trail in this dense forest so late in the afternoon?

Pathki had no answers. Her great fear of this man caused her to remain absolutely still. Cut Ears must not know she could see him. Several terror-filled minutes passed. The minutes seemed like hours. Pathki kept her eyes glued on Cut Ears.

Suddenly the stillness was broken by a loud screech-ing sound. It was the call of a bald eagle. It came from above the man and horse. No sooner had the eagle call ended than Cut Ears answered with the same call.

Someone's coming! thought Pathki. *Who? Why?* The girl's heart pounded like a hammer. She hardly dared to look but knew she must. She had to have answers. Some-thing told her she could be in great danger.

Only minutes later a strange man came into view. He walked right up to Cut Ears. The two men began speak-ing in a strange language. It was the same language Cut

Ears used to tell Pathki she was evil when she held the bow and arrow.

Pathki watched as the stranger handed Cut Ears a hide bundle. A few more words were spoken. Then Cut Ears gave the man the horse's lead rope. Quickly the man turned and disappeared with the horse back up the trail. Cut Ears immediately dropped to his knees on the trail. He opened the bundle to examine its contents.

The girl thought, *Cut Ears is the one! No enemy has been stealing our horses! Cut Ears betrays us! Now my people will know the answer to the mystery of the missing horses.* Only a few days before, Pathki had heard men in her village talk about the four horses lost in the past year. Most men thought that enemy warriors were stealing them. Now Pathki had the real answer and realized she had to get back to her people fast.

Pathki dared not move until Cut Ears left. She might make a sound to give her away. She had to keep her eyes on him every second so she would know when he was gone and which way he would go. Cut Ears had his back to Pathki. She could not see what he had in the hide bundle now spread out on the trail, so she wondered what the stranger had given for the horse.

Pathki saw Cut Ears retie the bundle and stand up. He turned to leave, heading back down the trail. Pathki took a deep breath. She felt an instant sense of relief. Just when she thought all was well, a squirrel in the tree above began a loud chattering. Pathki saw Cut Ears stop. She pulled her head behind the tree to be completely out of Cut Ear's view. The pesky squirrel chattered on and on.

Did Cut Ears see me? Is he coming? I must see. Ever so slowly, Pathki moved one eye past the tree. *Oh, no! Cut Ears has come back! He is looking this way!*

Pathki had to think fast. She said silently, "He must know I'm nearby. I have to leave this place. If the squirrel keeps chattering, Cut Ears will come looking. Stop, squirrel, stop!"

Quickly Pathki glanced around. Above and behind her were the dense bushes she had just avoided. She must head for the bushes, burrow into them. That would be her only chance.

Slowly Pathki turned and began a cautious move back toward the bushes. She kept the trees between herself and Cut Ears so he couldn't see her. Halfway to the safety of the bushes it happened; Pathki nearly stepped on a grouse. The terrified bird flew wildly through the trees to safety and startled the girl. The noise was alarming.

Pathki glanced back to look for Cut Ears. At the sound of the grouse, the huge man came scrambling uphill straight at the girl. Pathki's eyes caught Cut Ears' eyes for only a split second. Frantically the girl whirled around and ran straight up the mountainside.

"He saw me! He knows who I am! He knows I saw him sell our horse! I must get away! Run! Run!" she told herself.

Pathki used every ounce of her strength and all of her keen sense of balance to cross the downed timber as fast as possible. She ran like the wind. Her long hair flew straight behind her. Her arms moved up and down, helping her maintain perfect balance. A fall now would cause her to lose badly needed distance. Pathki kept her eyes glued to each log, always just ahead of her flying feet.

Cut Ears came across the timber at breakneck speed. With his powerful legs he gained on the small girl at an alarming rate. Before many more minutes had passed, the angry man would catch her.

"Faster! Faster! I must run faster! I can't let him catch me! Oh! What can I do? Run! Run!" The girl's great fear helped keep her going at top speed. The passing trees were just a blur. Pathki knew she was in a run for her life.

The horrified girl gasped for each breath. Her throat was dry. The steep climb over the downed timber sapped energy from Pathki's small body. Cut Ears was closing in on her. He was only fifty feet away. He drew his knife as he closed this gap. In less than two minutes he would have the helpless girl.

Don't look back! Pathki thought. Keep going! Just keep going! I hear him breathing! Oh! Don't let him catch me! Someone help me, please!

With Cut Ears only twenty-five feet away, Pathki came to a fallen tree propped up three feet above the ground. It was like a long shelf. One leap and Pathki was on top of this barrier. Instead of jumping down, the girl came to an abrupt stop. Right below her a startled black bear cub grunted and dashed for a nearby tree. He was on his way up the tree as Pathki hit the ground running. Ahead of her lay open space for the next one hundred feet.

Halfway across the open area Pathki heard a loud growl. Without stopping, she glanced back over her shoulder. She caught a glimpse of Cut Ears standing on the high log. Directly in front of him stood an angry black bear. The huge mother bear growled loudly. Her paws waved wildly not five feet from Cut Ears.

The surprised man dared not move. Pathki reached the trees and stopped to catch her breath. She looked back. The sow bear lunged at Cut Ears. The man turned and ran for his life.

This was the miracle Pathki needed. She darted into the trees and out of sight. Now she would use the fallen timber to hide her trail. She would leave no tracks on the logs. Every step she took would help her make it safely away from this dangerous man. Pathki hoped the angry bear could catch Cut Ears or at least chase him far enough to allow her to escape certain death.

On and on Pathki ran. She could hear nothing behind her. She began to feel that she had a chance after all.

Had a guardian spirit put the bears there to help her? A great feeling of comfort came over the desperate girl.

These good feelings didn't last. It took only a split second for disaster to strike. Pathki's foot hit a loose slab of bark. The bark slid forward, sending the girl falling between two logs. She felt a sharp tearing pain on her right shinbone. Next her right side slammed against a fallen tree as she dropped between the two logs.

Pathki ignored her pain. Adrenalin pumping into her veins and arteries helped her keep moving. To stop now could cause her to lose all the distance she had just gained. Running the logs was slower now. Another fall could stop her for good. A broken leg would mean the end.

Pathki glanced down at her right leg. A look of horror covered her face. Her leg was covered with blood. Worse yet, the blood was dripping onto the logs, leaving a trail easy for Cut Ears to follow.

What can I do? He'll find me for sure! I must stop the bleeding! How? I have to stop running! The trail of blood I'm leaving is a bad thing!

Pathki looked in every direction. Her eyes searched for a hiding place, a place to do something to stop the bleeding. She saw no safe place to stop. The bleeding girl ran on through the dense trees. As the loss of blood weakened the tired girl, her head began to spin with dizziness. If she kept going, she might faint. A fall could cause even greater injuries.

It was no use. Pathki had to stop. She jumped from a fallen tree to the ground. She slumped down, resting her back against a tree. She couldn't tell how bad the tear in her leg really was. The wound was covered with blood and dirt. Pathki began rubbing the blood and dirt from her shin. This caused a fiery pain. Pathki ground her teeth together as she continued to rub her leg with her hand. Soon the girl could see a flap of skin. The skin had been peeled upward during her fall. Pathki carefully pushed the flap of skin back over the scraped shinbone. In seconds the bleeding slowed down.

Quickly Pathki pulled the moccasin from her right foot and placed it over the tear. With its hide ties the girl secured the moccasin to her leg. She jerked a handful of long fringes from her deerhide dress and used these strands to make the bandage more secure. One strand she used to tie to the top of the makeshift bandage. This one she could hold in her right hand as she ran. It would help keep the clumsy bandage from slipping loose.

With her bandage complete, Pathki rose to her feet and ran on. She kept a close eye on her injured leg. No blood was reaching the logs. Pathki had to stop twice to tighten the ties, but she continued upward at a steady pace. She began to notice a sharp pain in her right side with every deep breath she took. Pathki ignored this pain.

The girl covered a difficult half a mile. A glance to her left caused her to make a sharp left turn. She could see an opening beyond the trees. She headed straight for the light. The opening revealed a large rock ledge angling upward. At the edge of this rock slab Pathki could look down on three more ledges below her.

The first ledge was fifteen feet down. It was a wide rock-strewn shelf. Below this first ledge were two more. Each ledge ran to the right at a slight uphill angle. At a place where Pathki could slide down loose rock, she made her way to the first ledge. She ran along the three-foot-wide ledge to her right for a short distance. Grabbing some scrub spruce trees, she lowered herself to the second ledge. In this same way she made her way to the final ledge and then ran to her right again.

Suddenly there it was, a perfect hiding place. The girl stood at a narrow opening in the rock wall. A tall vertical crack in the cliff went back for seven feet. Pathki squirmed into the crack as far as she could. She was out of breath. She couldn't have run much farther. All she could do now was wait. If Cut Ears found her, it would be over. At least now Pathki had a chance. The courageous girl had done all she could to save herself. She had to believe that her guardian spirit put the bears in Cut Ears' path at just the right time.

As Pathki sat far back in her narrow refuge, she began to breathe normally. It was time to plan her next move. She asked herself, *Will the horrible Cut Ears find me? Will he return tomorrow? I don't know. I do know my guardian spirit was with me today. What should I do next? How can I escape this evil man? How can I get back to my people? I must do the right thing. I must take the right path. For now, all I can do is wait.*

Pathki could never even imagine what unbelievable events lay just ahead. This desperate young Kootenai girl would need every ounce of strength and endurance just to stay alive in the next few days. Now all she could do was wait and hope.

5

Terrible Agony

Pathki made herself as comfortable as possible between the narrow rock walls. She looked straight ahead at the opening in the crevice. The afternoon sun was close to dipping behind the western mountains. The girl kept her ears tuned for any sounds of danger. Cut Ears could not get close to her without being heard on all the loose rock.

At the exact instant the sun slipped behind the western ridges, Pathki heard someone shouting from high above her. The girl pulled herself to her feet. Stiffly she shuffled to the opening in the crack.

"Girl! You escaped today! You won't escape tomorrow! I will find you! Then you die! I will find you!" Cut Ears' words echoed over the valley below. They sent a chill down Pathki's spine. The echoes made the words sound even more eerie and frightening.

Following Cut Ears' threatening words, all was still. The silence gave Pathki time to think. Her injured leg had stiffened and now burned with pain. Her badly bruised right side began to throb. Pathki moved back into her hiding place in the vertical crack. Before darkness made it impossible to see, the girl removed the crude bandage from her leg. Torn skin was matted with blood and dirt. Fresh blood still oozed from the edges of the skin flap.

Pathki did not dare move until dark. In the darkness she planned to walk north along the narrow ledge to a gully she had seen just beyond her hiding place. She had decided to go through that gully to the open slope below. From there Pathki could head for the trees and find a more comfortable place to hide for the night.

Darkness seemed to come slowly. The only sounds Pathki heard were birds singing their night songs. Moving in the darkness was tricky. The girl did not want to fall. A fall could start the bleeding all over again. Each deep breath caused a sharp pain in Pathki's right side. It seemed to be getting worse instead of better. She didn't know it, but two of her ribs were cracked. At the same time her leg continued to stiffen and burn with pain.

Pathki limped along to the waiting gully. She sat at the top of the steep depression in the rock. Holding her dress under her, she slid on her seat down over the loose sand and rock, steadying herself with her right hand.

It took Pathki twenty minutes to go less than eighty feet. Finally she reached the grassy slope. A half moon helped light her way to the trees. In the forest it was much harder to see. Pathki moved very slowly. Her steady pace led her deep into the dense forest. When she came to a spot where the forest floor was covered with a thick blanket of pine needles, Pathki slowly lowered herself to the soft covering. She could lie down only on her left side or on her back. Anything touching her right side caused her agonizing pain.

Pathki was exhausted, stiff, and painfully sore. It would be hard to get any sleep. Then her mind began racing. Somehow she had to think of a way to save herself from the evil Cut Ears. Somehow she had to find her way safely back to her people. Would anyone believe her story? Would Cut Ears find her before she could get home? A mistake could result in her death. It was hard for a confused girl in great pain to think of any way to solve this life-and-death dilemma.

Pathki tried to put all thoughts out of her mind and get some sleep. Sleeping would be difficult. Increasing pain allowed her to move only a little bit at a time. The pain made her desperate to find a position that would allow her to get some much-needed rest.

Hours had passed before Pathki finally dozed off for the first time. Yapping coyotes woke the girl from her restless sleep. Now the moving began all over again. The pain seemed to increase as the long night wore on. Doze off, wake up, move to ease the pain—doze off again—this cycle made the endless night seem like an eternity.

Songbirds woke Pathki at first light. As light filtered through the tall trees, the girl shivered in the chilly morning air. Pathki tried to rise to a sitting position. Her pain was so great, she dropped back down on her left side. Next she pulled her left leg under her body. Raising herself to her left knee, Pathki was able to rest her right hand against a leaning tree. With all her reserves she eased herself up to a standing position. Just standing there required all of the girl's effort. Her head ached. Her right side was tender and extremely sore. Her right shin throbbed and burned. Pathki's first steps were slow and unsteady.

Her thoughts raced: *Will I ever escape Cut Ears? If he comes now, I won't have a chance. Is he still up above? Are his eyes searching for me now? I must keep moving. I cannot go near our village now. He'll be waiting for me. Move! I must move far away. When I heal up, I'll think of a way to return. Now I must get far away from Cut Ears' eyes. I will do it today.*

It did not take long for Pathki to realize she could not go very far. Her pain was intense. Worst of all, she was weak and dizzy and had to stop often. She had gone only a short distance before she had to stop for good. She nearly passed out. Her eyesight became blurry. Her head spun like a top. Her stomach became queasy. Her legs shook beneath her.

Helplessly, Pathki stood leaning against a large tree. Her head was feverish. At the same time the girl began to shiver and shake violently. Pathki turned slowly to look back. She could see the north end of the rock ledges high above her. She hadn't made much distance. It would have to be enough. There was no use trying to go on.

Pathki had noticed clouds gathering over the valley. A light breeze caused her to shiver even more. She had eaten nothing for more than twenty-four hours. She was still exhausted from the restless night on the pine needles. Now the sky threatened rain any minute. Pathki knew she must find shelter. Shelter is always first in survival. Need for water would be next. Food could wait until later.

Now Pathki would have to use all her wisdom just to stay alive. She slowly moved down through the trees. Each step was painful and unsteady. The first thing she saw to give her some hope was a line of cottonwood trees on the valley floor. They always grow near a good water supply, so Pathki's eyes scoured the tree line. She could just barely make out the stream beyond the cottonwoods.

Pathki's knowledge of trees helped her discover this stream. Kootenai children learned fast from their elders. Like all children, Pathki had heard many stories around campfires on long winter nights. She had traveled every spring, summer, and fall as her people searched for food. Kootenai women knew where the first roots of spring could be found. Bitterroot was one of their favorites. It was found in a valley we now call the Little Bitterroot River Valley. There the bitterroot grows in very dry soil on the hillsides. Camas roots were dug later in the summer from damp meadows in the mountains.

Pathki was too sick and weak to eat anything. She turned back into the forest and moved slowly from tree to tree. Finally she saw the ideal place. Two trees lay parallel to each other. One was on the ground. The other was three feet above the forest floor. As a drizzling rain began, Pathki pulled four short poles to the two trees.

She used them to support a lean-to roof over the parallel logs. She covered this framework with pine boughs. It took her over an hour to complete the roof. Normally she could have done the work in fifteen minutes, but she was so weak she had to rest several times every minute.

Toward the end of her work, Pathki stumbled several times, almost falling. Sweat poured from her forehead. Her dress was soaked from the steady drizzle. With the lean-to roof finished, one more job remained. Now Pathki left the forest. On her hands and knees the weakened girl pulled bunches of grass. She made many agonizing trips back to her shelter with large amounts of grass. She was trying to fill the small space under the logs with the grass.

During her work gathering grass, she made one trip to the cottonwoods and the stream. Lowering herself to her left knee in the water, Pathki gulped down precious swallows of water. On her last trip for grass the shaky girl stumbled back to her lean-to shelter. Careful not to bump her painful right leg, Pathki crawled into her grass-filled shelter.

With grass making a nest, Pathki burrowed to the center of the pile. Grass below for a mattress and grass above for a blanket would help Pathki avoid the cold and dampness. Like a bird in a nest the weakened girl curled up for warmth.

Pathki still shook violently. Her head continued to burn with fever. Her right side ached. Her leg throbbed more than ever. The weakened girl faced another night of fitful sleep. Waking up often, the frail girl faced her misery bravely. Now her thoughts were very simple: *I will rest, sleep, drink water, stay hidden here, and somehow I will get better and be able to leave.*

The night was the worst one Pathki had ever known. She felt so miserable she thought maybe death would be a good thing.

Again, singing birds signaled the beginning of a new day. Pathki had slept only a little. She raised up on her left elbow. She stuck her head outside. The sun was already up. The rain had ended. Before the weakened girl could decide what to do next, she fell back onto her grass bed. She had used all her reserve strength to take her short look around. Now she just wanted to lie there.

A high fever gripped Pathki's small body. She could barely turn to find a more comfortable position. *What's the matter with me?* she thought. *I have no strength. I am so sick. I am so sick, I cannot leave here. I cannot leave.*

All day long Pathki lay in her shelter. She slept, woke up, and slept some more. Instead of getting better, the girl grew weaker and weaker. One day passed, then another long night, followed by another day. Time seemed to make the days and nights all run together. Pathki was getting badly dehydrated from lack of water. She needed water badly, but she kept putting off the necessary trip to the stream for the lifesaving liquid.

Several times Pathki reached down to rub her injured leg. Her first night on the pine needles she had removed the bandage for good. Now she could feel the swelling. Her leg was nearly twice its normal size. Her torn flesh had become infected. The infection had begun to spread throughout her body.

Pathki sensed she had to do something to help herself or she would die. With all the strength she had left, she pulled herself out into the sunlight. She sat slumped against her lean-to. When she looked at her injured leg, she was shocked at the sight of the horrible swelling. She had never seen anything like this. Her own leg caused her to turn her head. It looked hideous.

Water! She must make it to the water, which seemed to be her only answer. Without another thought Pathki prepared to make the agonizing trip to the stream. It was downhill all the way there. Still it would be a long and painful journey.

Pathki felt best lying on her back. With her good left leg she slowly pushed herself on her back downhill toward the water. Inch by inch she pushed on through the thick grass. She rested often. It took forty-five minutes to make the two hundred feet to the water. Pathki's heavy breathing made her ribs ache. Her misery was horrendous.

When Pathki's head slipped over the stream's bank, she paused only a few seconds before pushing herself down into the cool water. The water felt refreshing as it rolled over her thin frame. Pathki rested her head on a thick root that stuck out of the bank. She took a few seconds to catch her breath as she cupped her hands for drinking water. Her hands trembled as she drank the

precious liquid. It took lots of effort just to get the water to her dry lips. The water gave her only slight relief from her misery.

Once more Pathki took a look at her throbbing leg. A feeling of utter panic gripped the girl. The condition of her leg was worse than before. The swelling had traveled even higher up her leg. The swelling caused her skin to stretch and bulge grotesquely.

Pathki's head dropped back onto the large root. She had never felt more helpless. Would she die there, alone? What could this girl do to help herself now? Pathki had no way of understanding her medical needs. She had no idea that this infection was on its way through her entire body. If this infection was not stopped soon, it would end her short life.

How could Pathki know her true condition? How could she ever know what she needed to do to save herself? It seemed that only another miracle could save her now. The next few hours would decide her fate.

6

Guardian Spirit Acts

The pain in Pathki's leg increased more every second. She could hardly bear the excruciating pain. It would be this pain that would finally cause the young girl to do exactly what a modern-day doctor would do to save her life.

After thirty minutes in the water, Pathki pushed and pulled until she lay stretched out on the bank. Following a short rest on her back, the girl began the slow push back up to her hiding place. The water had refreshed her enough to help her move even better than during her trip down to the water.

On her way, beneath a large bushy tree, Pathki's left hand hit a thorn that had dropped from the tree. While she rested, the girl held the long sharp thorn between her thumb and first finger. As she stared at the thorn, her leg seemed to throb more violently than ever. Without even thinking, Pathki gripped the thorn as tightly as possible. She held it above her swollen leg. With one continuous motion she drove the thorn into the swelling and pulled it toward her.

Like an explosion, yellowish green pus spurted straight into the air. Pathki was startled by the great amount of poisonous fluid that gushed upward from her leg. The smell was sour and putrid. The pus splattered over her leg and the ground beneath. The throbbing ceased instantly. Lancing the wound was exactly what Pathki needed to do.

Without hesitating, the relieved girl turned on her back and pushed herself back to the creek. In the water she washed the awful pus away. Pathki already felt better, but she wasn't out of danger from the infection yet. In a sitting position in the water, the girl rubbed her infected leg with both hands. More pus oozed from the opening made with the thorn. Something told Pathki that getting this horrible liquid out of her leg was a must.

Pathki stayed in the creek until her wound was absolutely clean. Her leg had almost returned to its normal size. A great sense of relief had come over Pathki. While lying in the stream all that time, the girl's eyes had studied the bushes lining the banks. She could think more clearly now. She looked intently at the willow bushes. She realized that they, too, could help her. Kootenai women knew that many common plants contained healing powers. Pathki's mother and grandmother had taught her that willow twigs could help ease pain. Pathki had seen her mother and Quiet One chew on willow twigs to ease the pain of headaches and other discomforts. Today we know that willow twigs contain the same chemical used in making aspirin.

The willow twigs were another badly needed item. Pathki would do anything to ease her pain. She carefully rolled onto her hands and knees. Dipping her face directly into the water, she took one more drink. Pathki used the stream bank to help her struggle to her feet. She used her left hand to steady herself as she moved toward the willows.

After breaking off a large handful of twigs, Pathki climbed out of the water. She picked up a thick walking stick to steady herself. Still shaking from her ordeal, she took her first unsure steps back toward her shelter. Her legs became steadier with each step.

The cozy shelter looked better than ever to Pathki. She curled up inside and began chewing on her first willow twig. The afternoon sun had warmed her grassy nest. The water had tasted delicious. Her wound was clean. She felt much better but was still quite weak.

As Pathki chewed more and more willow twigs, her pain eased. She made several more trips to the creek before dark. That night the frail girl slept well. She only woke up three times. In the morning she rubbed her eyes as she sat upright in the opening in her shelter. Her leg looked better than ever. The miracle was happening. Her body was turning back the deadly infection. Now she had a good chance for a full recovery.

For the next two days Pathki stayed in her shelter. She only left to get water and to pick chokecherries and huckleberries. She slept off and on most of each day and night. When she was awake, she continued chewing the willow twigs. Every day she gained more strength.

Pathki began to plan her next move. She knew it was dangerous to remain in one place too long. It was time to move. After a final trip to the creek, Pathki was ready. The girl had just turned to leave the stream when she froze in her tracks. She caught a glimpse of something moving on the rocks above her. Whoever it was had knocked a rock loose, causing it to tumble down the mountainside.

Pathki ducked behind the willows. She had to think fast. *If it's Cut Ears, and he comes here to the stream, he'll find the path I wore in the grass. He'll find me for sure. I must leave this place.*

Pathki knew that parts of the creek could be seen from above, but the stream would hide her trail. There would be no tracks in water for Cut Ears to follow, so the stream was still her best escape route.

Instantly Pathki dropped to her knees in the water. She lowered herself to her stomach. Hugging the bank, the girl began pulling herself north and upstream. The bank would hide her from view. Once she was out of sight of the rocks, she would walk fast upstream and away from danger.

There was much less pain in Pathki's side. The painkiller in the willow twigs had helped greatly. Still, moving on her stomach was slow. The rocks in the creek were wet and slippery. Every few yards Pathki raised her head to see if the ledges were still visible. She had to travel quite a distance before she could even see the rocks. Her first glimpse of the rocks gave her only a limited view. Her second look sent a chill through her body. There he stood in plain sight! Cut Ears was right there. Pathki was sure he was looking right at her. *He sees me! He must!* she thought with horror.

Quickly the girl lowered her head. She pressed her body against the bank. She glanced around, searching for a place to hide. She saw no place at all. If Cut Ears came, he would find her easily. Her only chance was to keep going along the creekbed.

Cut Ears stayed on his perch high above, searching for any sign of the girl. Pathki realized that he had not seen her yet. After being chased by the bear, Cut Ears had returned to the village to watch for Pathki's return. Once back at the village, Cut Ears told a terrible lie. He said he had seen a giant grizzly kill Pathki and carry her away. He even told the people how he did everything he could to save the girl from this awful death.

Cut Ears made up the story so no one would go out to search for the lost girl. Then Cut Ears planned to find Pathki himself before she could get back to the village. In a short time the people would leave and move their village to the camas root digging grounds. If her people ever saw Pathki again, they would think she was returning from the spirit world.

Pathki made good time along the creekbed. Her side still bothered her a little. She ignored it. Every second counted. The girl didn't see Cut Ears again. She just kept moving.

Ahead, the creek flowed from a wide meadow filled with grass and willow bushes. At this place Pathki crawled out of the creek and into the thick bushes. She stood in the tall bushes and looked back toward the ledges. They were completely out of her view. The girl pushed her way through the dense willows. Suddenly she broke through to a game trail made by moose and deer. The animals had traveled this trail often. It was perfect for Pathki. Now she could move much faster and still remain completely hidden.

At the end of the large meadow, Pathki disappeared into the forest. Now she found herself moving upward once more. The girl took advantage of the downed trees to avoid leaving a trail. Pathki was still not back at full strength. Eating berries and drinking lots of water had helped, but it wasn't enough. The young girl's body had gone through a great ordeal. Now Pathki would use her remaining strength to escape her deadly enemy again.

Just when Pathki thought she couldn't take another step, she saw the trees thin out a short distance ahead. She had no idea where she was. The girl headed out of the trees into the clearing. Her eyes feasted on the sight above her. She was looking at the exact spot where she had stood not long before. She remembered the great view from that rocky point.

Pathki was tempted to head up to the place she had picked to seek her guardian spirit. She knew that would be too dangerous now. To stand there would put her out in the open where Cut Ears could see her easily.

The girl made her plan quickly. She circled beneath the rocky point, staying hidden in the trees. She headed north in the direction of the distant lake that she had seen from that summit above her.

Meanwhile, Cut Ears found Pathki's tracks to the stream. He found her makeshift lean-to. He could not find any tracks to show him which way the girl had gone. For now Pathki had made a perfect escape.

The desperate girl traveled steadily for two days. She stopped only to pick berries and drink water. Each night she made a mattress, using spruce branches. She used some of them to cover herself. Pathki still chewed willow twigs as she walked. Her hunger for fish and game meat grew with each passing hour. At the top of the ridge just ahead, a great surprise awaited the hungry girl.

The first sign of this surprise was a loud crashing sound. Pathki quickly crouched behind a large tree. The sound grew louder and louder. Whatever was making all the noise was coming right at her. The girl was sure it must be a large animal. She didn't need to wait long to learn she was right.

A huge bull elk came crashing through the nearby trees. The animal stopped directly in front of the hiding girl. The animal's coat was lathered with sweat. Foam covered the animal's jaws. Its tongue hung from the side of its mouth.

Suddenly the elk realized that Pathki was hiding close by. The confused animal stood for an uncertain few seconds, deciding which way to run. As the exhausted elk turned to leave, Pathki could see the animal's right side. Its whole flank was streaked with blood. Two arrows were embedded in its body. The weakened animal crashed on through the trees, leaving the startled girl behind.

Hunters! There are hunters in this forest! Pathki knew exactly what to do. She thought all she had to do was wait. The hunters would be coming to find the wounded animal. They would find Pathki. She would be safe. She could tell her story. Cut Ears would be found out.

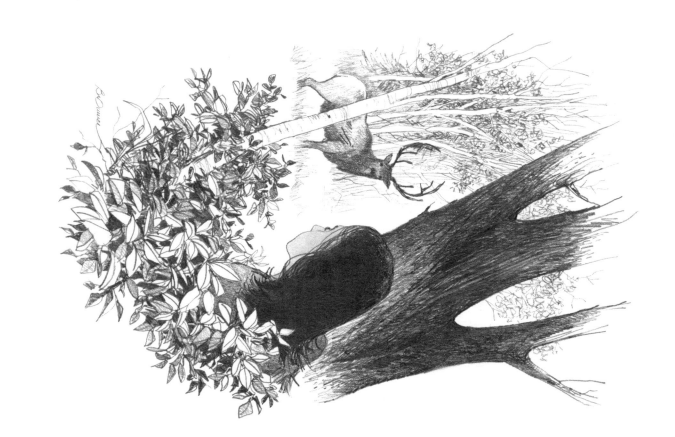

The excited girl waited anxiously, expecting the hunters any minute. Time passed. No one came. Where were the hunters? How far had the wounded animal traveled with the deadly arrows in his body? Pathki didn't have any answers.

After a long wait, the girl knew that no hunters had followed this elk. Now only a few hours of daylight remained. Pathki acted fast. She picked up the trail of blood and followed the dying animal.

Twenty minutes later the girl sensed she was close. Not far ahead, Pathki found a broken arrow shaft. A large pool of blood had soaked the pine needles at the girl's feet. Only thirty feet farther, Pathki came to the body. The bull elk's painful struggle had ended.

The girl wasted no time. She pulled the good arrow from the animal's hide. She used it to loosen the broken one. Finally she had freed both of them. The arrowheads were the tools she needed. The sharpest point was on the broken shaft. It would make the better knife.

Pathki wanted two things from this surprise gift. The large hide would be very valuable. It could serve as a shelter or for a bed. The second thing the girl wanted very badly was fresh meat. She would take only what she could carry. Pathki had lots of work to do in a short time. When darkness came, the dead animal would attract wolves, bears, and other hungry meat eaters. The girl would need every minute of daylight left to do her grizzly work.

Pathki went right to work. The arrow point was sharp but very small. This would be a big job. The young girl had never skinned a large animal before. She had watched her mother and other women as they skinned deer. She tried to remember exactly how they did it.

Pathki's hands moved quickly to do the messy work. The arrow point worked fine at first, but it wasn't very good for cutting through the hide around the neck and the legs. Soon the point began to loosen as a result of the tremendous pressure Pathki put on it. She quickly switched to the other arrow. It loosened even sooner. Before long, both arrowheads had come off their shafts. Pathki had to finish the skinning work by holding the sharpest arrow point between her fingers. The work was slower than ever now. Darkness was closing in on the girl.

In near darkness Pathki finally pulled the hide from the huge animal. The hide was wet and very heavy. In minutes the girl had two slabs of meat cut from the elk's hindquarters. Next she scraped fat from the animal's spine. She stuffed the fat into one of her moccasins. She needed the fat to tan the hide. She didn't have time to retrieve the elk's brain. The brain would have been the best for tanning, but the fat would have to do.

As Pathki worked, she remembered the location of the finest meat of all. Inside the body cavity along the backbone lay the tenderloin muscle. It would be tender and delicious. Kootenai people did not like raw meat, but Pathki was so hungry that this warm tender meat would taste good, especially after she became used to it.

With the precious meat rolled safely in the hide, the girl shouldered her load and headed off in the darkness. She knew she should get a safe distance from the elk carcass. She would find a good place to spend the night. The next day Pathki would have lots of work to do. First she would cut the meat in thin strips and hang it in the sun to dry. Next she would scrape the elkhide clean and use the fat to rub into the hide to soften it.

As Pathki moved along, she began to think about all that had happened. The girl had been taught that there was a meaning in everything that happened in life. What did the gift of the elk mean? Was her guardian spirit giving her the hide and the meat for a reason? Was it to tell her to stay in the forest and not return to her village yet? What did it all mean? Pathki could only wonder about it all.

Pathki would think many thoughts in the days ahead. Many more questions would fill her mind. When this amazing adventure would end, Pathki's life would never be the same again.

7

Majestic Love

Rolled up in her new elkhide bed, Pathki slept well. She was up early the next morning and anxious to start drying the meat and scraping the hide. A wonderful surprise greeted the girl as she rolled from her bed. She heard sounds of ducks just below her. Pathki walked a short distance to her right to investigate. There it was! Right below her lay the beautiful lake she had seen from the distant summit days before. This was another gift from her guardian spirit. She knew it. Water was critical to her survival.

The excited girl went right to work while chewing on bits of tenderloin. She used the sharp arrowheads to slice the elk meat into thin strips. Soon she had all the meat laid out on a smooth log to dry in the sunlight.

On her first trip to the lake Pathki searched for a flat rock. She needed just the right rock to use as a scraper. It didn't take long to find a perfect rock. An outcropping of slate-like rock lay along the shoreline of the lake. The thin slabs would be excellent scrapers. Now the work would go much faster.

Pathki's plan was forming. She would finish her work on the hide. She would stay near the lake for a few days, eating and resting. When her strength returned, she would start to work her way back to her people.

Pathki decided to camp in a different place each night. Moving would be more work, but it would make it harder for Cut Ears to find her. The girl always walked on downed trees or thick pine needles. She did not want to leave any tracks for the man to see. Every trip to the lake, the clever girl was careful to avoid walking in grass or dirt. Near the lake she walked on rocks or in dense bushes. She never stayed at the water's edge very long.

Before going out into the open, Pathki's eyes searched the ridges above the lake for any sign of trouble.

Pathki's eyes also studied every detail of the lake. The deep blue water was beautiful and so peaceful. The lake was over a mile long and half a mile wide at the widest place. Several islands dotted the lake's surface. The islands were small and covered with grass, bushes, and small trees. Two majestic trumpeter swans were using one small island for a nesting place. Many ducks had picked this lake for their summer home.

After scraping the hide clean, Pathki went on an exploration of her surroundings. She located good places to hide in case of danger. She found a plentiful supply of huckleberries, chokecherries and other edible plants. There were also many thistle plants whose stems and roots she could eat.

On Pathki's second day at the lake, she climbed to the top of the highest ridge above the lake. On this high spot on the west ridge, Pathki could look down into a narrow river valley. She did not recognize this valley. She had no way of knowing that her people had visited this river often. They fished on this river many miles downstream.

The very size of the river told Pathki there had to be people on it somewhere. It had to be used for fishing and canoe travel.

Pathki had a strange feeling come over her as she gazed at the river far below. Somehow she knew this river held the key to her safe return to her people. Thoughts and questions filled the girl's mind. *How will this river help me? What does the river tell me, oh, guardian spirit?* Suddenly Pathki felt a sudden urge to get back to her camp. She wanted to begin to pack her meat away. She was ready to start for home.

A rush of joy came over Pathki as she traveled down the ridge. She said, "I will start for home tomorrow. The river is my answer." The girl felt a strong urge to follow her feelings about the river. Her excitement made her tingle all over. She was going home!

Pathki was still careful to stop several times on her way down the ridge. She looked in every direction for signs of danger. She knew she had to remain alert. She must be alert for any sound or unusual movement. A mistake now could ruin everything.

At one stop Pathki had a good overview of the small island below and the trumpeter swan's nest. She watched the mother swan rise to her feet. With her long white neck the graceful swan gently pushed her head under each large white egg. She carefully turned the four eggs over one at a time. This turning would help keep the babies inside warm on all sides. Pathki also noticed the father swan close by. He stood on the far side of the small island near the shoreline.

Pathki moved on. She thought about the mother swan's love and care of her four eggs. The girl remembered her own mother and her love for her. Tears came to Pathki's eyes as she remembered Quiet One's words: "Your mother held you close. We could not stop her bleeding. The Spirit removed her to the spirit land. Before she took her last breath, she asked us to love you and to care for you."

As Quiet One's words passed through Pathki's mind, the girl spoke aloud: "Quiet One, I'm coming home. Somehow I will find a way to make it back. My guardian spirit is powerful. My body has healed. I have been given food, water, and shelter. Cut Ears will never get me. His spirits are weak. I'm coming back to you."

Pathki spoke these words softly. The words made her feel better. Her tears stopped. For a moment her thoughts caused her to forget exactly where she was headed. She realized she had gone out of her way.

The girl stopped instantly. She noticed a movement along the lakeshore. Pathki jumped behind a clump of bushes. Coyote! It was a coyote slowly moving in the direction of the trumpeter swan's island. Pathki watched intently. She knew the coyote's purpose. He was after the swan's eggs.

The young coyote moved very deliberately in a crouched position. The animal stayed as low as he could. The closer he came to the island, the slower he moved. Pathki could tell that the swans knew nothing about the approaching danger. The mother swan couldn't even see the shoreline where the coyote stalked toward her. The father swan was too far away to see the enemy. Pathki would soon witness one of the most dramatic events ever seen in the animal world. In the next few minutes she would witness a life-and-death struggle that she would never forget.

The coyote's plan was working perfectly. He reached the shoreline directly across from the island. Being an excellent swimmer, the coyote could paddle through the water the thirty feet to the island in just a few minutes. Once on the island he planned to drive the mother swan from her nest and devour the helpless eggs.

Without hesitation the coyote slid into the water and swam for the island. Only the animal's head stuck above the surface. He cut through the water silently.

All went well for the coyote until two startled ducks splashed away in a noisy takeoff from the lake's surface. Before the coyote knew what was happening, the father swan entered the lake and rounded the corner. Seeing the treacherous coyote, the giant swan spread its great wings. With its webbed feet paddling wildly, the angry swan beat the air with its powerful wings and rose into the air three feet above the lake's surface.

Pathki watched in utter amazement as the mighty swan flew on a direct course toward the swimming coyote. The great bird reached the coyote and went into a

dive. The coyote was caught by surprise. The forty-five–pound swan landed on the middle of the coyote's back. The bird clamped its powerful beak on the coyote's neck and drove its head under the water.

Pathki could not believe the power of the swan. No sooner had the male swan hit his target than here came the mother swan. She came splashing into the fight. The mother swan drove her beak into the coyote's fur and shoved him even deeper into the lake.

The furious battle lasted only minutes. Pathki never saw the coyote surface even once during the one-sided struggle. The determined swans held the coyote under until he drowned. The coyote didn't have a chance. The power and fury of the two mighty birds had protected their four precious eggs.

The mother swan was the first to leave the scene. She calmly returned to her nest. The father swan stayed. He floated on the surface, guarding the spot of the fight. Soon the dead coyote floated to the surface and drifted away. The male swan followed closely as if to make sure the coyote had no life left.

Never in her life had Pathki seen anything like this. Now she understood better than ever how much even wild animals love their young ones. Yes, the trumpeter swans stood ready to fight to the death to protect their babies. Even an animal's love is a wonderful and powerful thing.

Pathki watched as the coyote's body drifted toward the shore. Finally the father swan realized the coyote was no longer a threat. He turned and swam back to the island. He would be ready for the next threat that might come.

The coyote's body snagged on a dead tree lying submerged near the lakeshore. Pathki made her way to that spot. She entered the water and waded to within arms' reach of the dead animal. She freed the body from the snag and pulled the animal from the water. She laid it in the thick grass.

Pathki realized this was another gift from her guardian spirit. The hide would be very useful. Even the meat could be eaten if the girl had nothing else.

Once more the arrowheads were needed. Pathki went right to work skinning the coyote. She also cut away the animal's tendons and other cord-like parts of the coyote's body. These strands of sinew would be used for sewing. The small hide could be used as a storage bag for her food supply.

Back at her campsite Pathki scraped the hide clean. She used the little fat she had to soften it as much as possible. She used small bones as awls. With the sharp bones she punched holes into the coyote's hide for easy sewing. Other small bones served as needles.

Pathki felt better than ever. Her body had healed. She had her elkhide, the coyote storage bag, a rock scraper, and two sharp arrowheads. She had taken care of herself amazingly well. Now her mind turned to thoughts of her people. Her heart ached with loneliness. Oh, how Pathki longed to see Two Birds, Red Willow, Quiet One, and her whole family. *Where are they now?* the girl wondered. *What about Cut Ears? Can I make it back to my people before he finds me? Will my guardian spirit be with me all the way back to my people? I will try. Tomorrow I start for home.*

Pathki knew her first task would be to find the best route home. If her people had moved, she would have to find out where they were. That night she lay awake for a long time making her plans. Her excitement grew with every thought about her trip. She knew it would be a dangerous attempt to get to her people before Cut Ears got to her.

Once again Pathki's sleep was very restless. She woke up often. Each time she started thinking about her exciting plans. It was hard to get back to sleep. She seemed to be awake most of the night.

Just before dawn Pathki was up and busy getting ready to leave the lake. Her plan would take her over the western ridge and down the mountainside to the river far below. She planned to find a safe place to camp near the stream. From this camp she would explore the river in both directions. When she found the best route to take, Pathki would move on.

The girl was filled with excitement. *I'm going home!* she thought. *I will see my mother and Quiet One soon! I will tell them my story! They will believe me. My guardian spirit is with me. Cut Ears will never find me. I will make it.*

Shouldering her heavy load, Pathki circled the north end of the lake in the early morning light. Even the climb to the top of the western ridge was easier than expected. At the top the girl paused to scan the valley below for possible danger. Her eyes took in every detail. To her left and south the river made a big bend and disappeared from view. To her right the river came from the north, flowing from a narrow gorge in the rock cliffs. In all, she could see less than half a mile of the river.

Pathki took her time scanning the scene in all directions. Her trip down was a steep one. She took her time to avoid a fall. At a place two hundred feet above the river, the girl found a perfect place to make camp. A large spruce tree had toppled over in a strong wind. The tree's root system raised up to a vertical position. It created a wall of roots, dirt, and rock and had left a hole three feet deep.

Pathki stepped into the hole behind the root system. She threw the rocks from the hole. With her foot she leveled the soil. Next she collected pine boughs and created a mattress on the smooth soil. If bad weather came, Pathki could quickly make a lean-to roof. It was the perfect place for a shelter and was set safely back from the river.

Before dark Pathki made her first trip to the river's edge. The bank on her side was steep. On the opposite side a gravel bar ran along for a hundred feet. Pathki walked upstream only a short distance to a place where she could climb down the bank to get water. On her way there the girl stopped. She noticed a family of river otters swimming along the opposite shore. She watched the two adult otters dive below the surface and come back up with fish in their jaws. The two otters darted upstream with their catch. The two smaller ones were not far behind.

Pathki was very hungry for fish. Her meat supply was almost gone. When she had time she would try her hand at fishing. Pathki had no way of knowing that this otter family would have their own surprise for this Kootenai girl. They would give her a gift that would change her people's lives for the better. The otters would send Pathki home with a great gift for all Kootenai people. The next few days would be remembered by Pathki for the rest of her life.

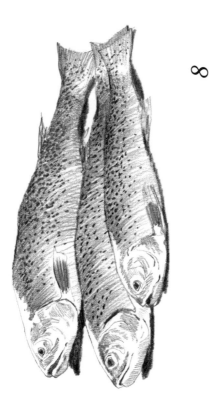

8

Amazing Discovery

That night Pathki slept soundly until a rumble of thunder woke her. Distant lightning flashes lit up the sky. The girl had a supply of poles lying next to her camp. She had planned to use them to construct a roof the next day. Now there was no waiting for daylight. Quickly Pathki leaned the poles against the vertical wall of roots. She used pine boughs from her mattress to make a roof, then hurried to nearby trees to get more.

After speedily completing her roof, Pathki ducked inside to avoid the rain that came pouring down. She rolled up in her elkhide. Fortunately the dense forest protected her from the strong winds. Between the crashing rolls of thunder, Pathki could hear the trees squeaking and groaning as they rubbed against each other. A few dead trees came smashing down very close by.

Instead of passing by quickly, like most thunderstorms, this one went on and on. The wind shifted and held the clouds over the entire river valley. Daylight came and the storm continued all morning. The thunder and lightning came and went, but Pathki would wait out the storm in her cozy shelter. Some water dripped through her roof, landing harmlessly on the elkhide.

The anxious girl could hardly wait for the storm to end. This was supposed to be her first day of exploration. She had hoped to learn something from a trip upstream that day. The girl knew she had to be patient. Lightning was very dangerous, and a falling tree could kill. All the noise made it difficult to hear any danger. Waiting was hard to do but very necessary.

Late in the afternoon the storm finally broke up and moved east. The skies overhead cleared. The wind stopped. Water still dripped from the tall pines. Pathki had time for a trip upstream and a short look around. She headed north, glad to be walking again.

Just a short distance upstream, Pathki saw the otter family again. All four animals were playing near some large rocks sticking out of the water. The girl was amazed at the speed of these creatures. She watched them for several minutes. They seemed to be playing a game of hide and seek. When Pathki came closer, the otters stopped their play to stare up at her. When she did nothing to bother them, they began playing again as if she wasn't even there.

Pathki left the otter family to their play. She continued upriver to the deep gorge she had seen from above. She avoided staying in the open very long because she was still worried about being seen by Cut Ears. There was only enough time to climb the ridge above the gorge. Satisfied with what she was able to find out, the girl turned and started back toward her camp.

Just before leaving the river, Pathki climbed down the riverbank and took a long drink of water. As she looked up from her drink, she spotted the otter family again. Strangely enough, the two adult otters swam to exactly

the same place in the river as they had gone to the night before. Once again they dove below the surface. Again each otter surfaced with a fish in its mouth. This was a curious thing to see happen two nights in a row and in the very same place. Pathki realized that these two otters knew how to fish and where to fish.

That night Pathki dreamed about the otters. In her dream the otters dove for fish and came swimming to her to share their catch. When she tried to reach for the fish, the otters playfully swam away. The smaller ones laughed at her and hollered, "Chase us, chase us." It was a strange, strange dream indeed.

The next morning dawned clear and bright. The forest smelled fresh and new after the soaking rain. Pathki was on her way early. She headed downstream this time. It didn't take her long to reach the big bend in the river. On her side the bank became very steep and difficult to walk. Going was hard and very slow.

Finally, after two hours of strenuous travel, Pathki came to a dead end. Right in front of her stood a steep rock wall more than two hundred feet high. The bank on the opposite side was gentle and easy to travel. This would be the place to cross the river and continue south on the west side.

Pathki stood a long while in deep thought. Her plan had to be made that day. She needed to decide which way to go and then get moving. She was tired of waiting, but the girl knew her decision could mean success or failure.

On her way back to her camp, Pathki made her final plan. She wouldn't leave too soon. She planned to take one more day to explore upstream. Unless she found something to the north to convince her that was the best direction, she would head south the day after. Pathki would walk to the rock wall, cross the river, and head south. She hoped that somehow she would pick the right direction.

Pathki was excited to have her plan made. Now it wouldn't be long before she would be on the move again. As she walked back to her camp, she had no idea that the otter family would cause a change in her plan. There was a great surprise waiting for Pathki before her day ended. In fact, this was the day this Kootenai Indian girl would discover something that would make the lives of her people better than ever.

About the same time as the day before, Pathki went to the river's edge for water. There they were again, the otter family swimming to the same spot in the river. Pathki watched them very closely. She knew what they were going to do even before they did it. She was right. The two adult otters dove under and came up with their fish. The most curious thing about this happening three days in a row was that it was always done in exactly the same place.

Pathki didn't go right back to her shelter. She just sat on the riverbank, staring at that special place in the river. Minutes later the otters returned. Again they dove. Again they surfaced with fish. After doing it the third time, the otters left and did not return.

Pathki's curiosity was running wild. *How do the otters do it? Why do they dive in the same place every day? Why are there always fish there for the otters? Why can't the fish escape?* The girl had lots of questions and no answers. She just sat there, wondering about all this.

Pathki was nearly out of meat. She had been eating mostly roots and berries. If the otters could catch so many fish in the same special spot, maybe she could, too. She decided to make a hook from the sharp coyote bones she had saved. With a grasshopper for bait and sinew for fishing line, the girl would drop her hook in the special place and try her luck. If she could catch a few fish, the meat could be used for her trip home. She had no idea how long it would take to find her people. A supply of fish would be a good thing to have with her. She would go fishing the next morning.

In early morning light the girl crossed the river downstream so as not to disturb the fishing hole. The morning crossing was refreshing and easy. The dripping-wet girl climbed from the water and went straight to the otters' fishing spot. With a squirming grasshopper on her homemade hook, Pathki dropped her line into the water. A tug came instantly. The girl pulled back on her line to haul in her catch. The line stopped dead. It was securely snagged on something in the deep pool of water.

Pathki dropped to her hands and knees on the bank. She reached into the current to free the snag. Her hand found a submerged willow bush which held her hook securely. Using all her strength, Pathki pulled the bush upward. To her surprise the willow bush seemed unusually heavy. As the bush broke the surface, the girl could look into the branches. She could hardly believe her eyes. There were fish trapped inside the willow stems. *How could this be? How could this willow bush hold fish?*

Pathki dropped her fishline and quickly slid her hands down the branches. She reached deeper into the water. Grabbing the upper end of the branches, the girl squeezed them all together. This kept the fish held tightly in the crude trap.

Next Pathki slid her feet right into the stream. Standing next to the willow bush, she was able to lift the whole bush and shove it onto the bank. She jumped onto the bank and pulled the bush safely away from the water. Pathki knelt down and pulled the branches apart. Three beautiful fish flopped about in the grass.

Pathki's heart pounded with excitement. She had discovered the otters' secret. Now she had to find out how the willow bush could trap fish. She knew what she had to do. She took the bush back to the water and lowered it back in. She was very careful to lay the bush in exactly the same position it was in when she had found it. The root end faced upstream, allowing the branches to flex with the gentle current. Pathki could see that a beaver had eaten off all the stems at about the same height. Only five feet of the willow bush remained attached to the root system, which was wedged between two large rocks.

With the willow trap in the water, the girl quickly gathered up the three fish. Using her sharp arrowheads, Pathki cleaned her catch. Each one weighed over one pound. The girl was very hungry for fish but did not dare make a fire. Any smoke could be seen easily, and Pathki was still worried about Cut Ears finding her. She would take no chances with fire. The best she could do would be to cut the fish into thin strips and dry the meat in the sun. She was not hungry enough to force herself to eat raw fish.

Pathki checked the willow bush before she started back across the river. She raised it to the surface for a look. It was still empty. As she held it below the surface for a few minutes, she watched the branches wave gently in the current. She imagined how a fish swimming upstream could enter the open branches. Once between these willow stems, the fish would reach the roots that blocked its way. The frantic fish would desperately search for an escape route. The fish did not or could not turn around to swim out the way it had come.

Pathki had learned the secret of the otters. Now she knew why this was their favorite fishing hole. The animals were using their intelligence to help themselves to an easy catch. Like the otters, Pathki, too, would return to this unique trap for more fish. For now she would head back to her camp with the gift of the three fish.

Before entering the water again, Pathki began to think out loud: "Mother, Quiet One, I'm coming home. I will be safe. My guardian spirit is with me. I was given the elk and the coyote. I was given tools for my work. Now I have been given fish. The otters have been my teachers. Great swans have shown me love, courage, and power. I have learned much. Now my guardian spirit will protect me from Cut Ears. I am coming home. I know I can make it."

Pathki spoke softly as she crossed the shallow river. She headed straight to her camp. Her plans would change. She would not explore upstream. Pathki would use the next day to dry her fish and rest. She had an unexplained feeling that going south was the answer. Pathki would also check the trap one more time before leaving. The girl tingled with excitement. The thought of heading for home made it seem as if time was crawling until the moment to leave would come.

The last day at the river camp passed very slowly. Pathki cut pieces of elkhide to place inside her moccasins. This would cushion the bottom of her feet for the long trip home. All day long the girl turned the thin strips of fish meat as they dried in the sunlight. Pathki was thankful for the heat of the sun.

As Pathki did her chores, she kept her eyes on the opposite shore. She couldn't see the submerged willow bush. She wondered if there were any fish trapped in it yet. The impatient girl made several trips to the river and upstream to the otters' favorite spot. On the last walk she saw the adult animals sunning themselves on the rocks. The two young otters were wrestling on a large flat slab of rock.

Pathki watched the otters long enough to see all four of the animals join in the play. Soon the frisky animals were diving into the water, circling the rocks, racing over the tops of the rocks, sliding back into the water, as they played their games of tag and hide and seek.

Pathki witnessed the great speed of the otters and saw how much they enjoyed playing together. She noticed their sparkling eyes. She had never seen animals so carefree and happy. Oh! How Pathki longed to be happy and safely back with her family. As she watched the otter family, she promised herself that she, too, would find happiness among her people.

That afternoon Pathki made her trip to check the willow trap once more. It had worked again. This time four fish were hopelessly trapped among the willow stems. She left the fish there for the otter family and hurried back to her camp.

At sundown the girl enjoyed some strips of dried fish meat. She packed the rest of the meat in her coyote bag. Excitement about leaving for home made it hard for her to get to sleep and stay asleep. The days ahead would be a great test of this girl's strength, wisdom, and courage. They would be a time of excitement, high adventure, and fear. Pathki was ready for anything the future had in store for her.

9

Dangerous Delay

In the early morning light a faint mist rose from the river's surface. There was barely enough daylight to see, but Pathki headed south. With everything rolled into the elkhide, she carried all of her treasures on her back. At the steep rock cliff the girl cautiously stepped into the rocky river and began wading toward the opposite shore. Her trip home was well underway.

As the sun dipped into the river valley, Pathki stayed in the trees a short distance back from the river. She walked as quietly as possible. Her ears were tuned to any sound that might signal trouble coming. She didn't want anything to go wrong because of her carelessness. Gradually the narrow river valley began to widen. The trees were not as dense, and there were more meadows and open spaces. The soil was much drier. Sagebrush grew in the open places and up the hillsides.

Pathki knew she could be seen much easier in these open areas. Wherever possible, the girl went out of her way to stay in the trees or bushes. By now the sun was high overhead. Pathki began to tire. Sweat poured from her body. She had not walked for half a day straight for a long time. In her excitement to go as far as possible, the girl had failed to even stop for a drink of water. Pathki knew she had to stop for a rest. Water and food would revive her. This was the time to pause for water and a snack from her supply of berries and dried fish meat.

After a long drink of water from a bubbling spring, Pathki crawled into a dense bush growing against a large boulder. Hidden in the shady bush and with the boulder for a backrest, she enjoyed her meal. The girl ate, rested, and began thinking. *Am I going the right way? Should I have gone upstream instead? When will I know?*

Doubts poured through Pathki's mind. She sat staring at her elkhide and her coyote bag. She began daydreaming about home, about her mother, about Quiet One, about Red Willow, and about all her people. Suddenly and strangely, a calmness came over her. Something inside her seemed to be telling her she was headed in the right direction. Pathki would never be able to explain this eerie calmness, but she knew it was a powerful feeling. She would continue south.

Early that afternoon Pathki glanced at the mountains on the opposite side of the river. There on the eastern ridge she saw a scene that caused her to stop for a longer look. Her eyes were attracted to a low saddle of rock. The slope leading to this dip in the ridge looked very gradual. A line of trees led up the ridge. The saddle looked mysteriously inviting to Pathki. It would be an easy climb and would give the girl a good view east. The more she thought about it, the more Pathki was attracted to that place on the ridge. It was almost like a magnet pulling the girl upward.

After a quick crossing of the river, Pathki began her climb to the saddle. It wasn't as easy as it looked. The girl's heavy load pulled against her shoulders. On her final rest stop below the saddle, Pathki thought she heard sounds. She tuned her ears to try to sort out the faint noises.

Off Pathki ran, forgetting how tired she was, forgetting the load she carried. As she rushed toward the saddle, the sounds became louder and louder. Many people were shouting, hollering, and banging sticks together.

Pathki arrived on the saddle completely out of breath. Stretching below her to the east lay a long valley sprinkled with spruce and aspen trees. Boys, young men, and older men were spread out all along both side ridges. All of them were shouting while they beat two sticks together to add to the noise. Pathki was witnessing a surround. A deer drive was underway. The men and boys had encircled a large herd of deer. They were forcing the frantic animals down the narrow valley. The deer would be driven through the narrowest place between the two ridges. Here the armed hunters were waiting. Their bows were ready. Each had a quiver full of arrows ready to fire. The success of this drive would provide hundreds of pounds of meat for the village. All the hides would be taken. Antlers would be fashioned into many different tools. Every part of these animals would be useful.

Pathki's eyes took in the entire scene. The men and boys raced along the side hills, making sure the deer kept moving. Others ran directly behind the animals, making them bound down the valley toward the waiting hunters. It was like herding the desperate animals through a giant funnel.

Who were these people? Pathki could only wonder. She was too far away to tell. Most of the men and boys were out of the girl's sight already. Before she could think of what to do next, Pathki saw something that startled her. One runner on the south ridge had taken a very bad fall. The girl expected him to jump up and keep going. Instead he lay perfectly still. Pathki watched for several minutes. She saw no movement from the fallen one. She realized she was the only witness to this accident. All the other runners had disappeared down the valley, not knowing one of their own was badly injured.

Pathki was confused. Many questions flooded her mind. *What should I do? Who are these people? How badly is this person hurt? Should I go down to help? Could these be my people? Could Cut Ears be close by?*

Pathki remembered when she was helpless like this fallen one. There was no one to help her. She had to help herself. In her misery, help seemed to come from unexpected places. She had found the thorn to release the poisonous pus from her swollen leg. The willow twigs gave her the chemical to kill her pain and fever. The elk came to her at exactly the right time. The arrowheads were there for tools. The coyote hide was a gift, too. Just a few days ago she had learned the otters' secret of finding fish.

Pathki knew she was brought to this spot at just the right time. Now she could give a person in need a gift of her own. Maybe the Spirit brought her to this place just in time to see this accident.

Down from the saddle the girl rushed. Pathki angled to her right, taking a straight route to the injured one. The shouts of the deer chasers had faded away. The girl arrived at the scene of the fall in a matter of minutes. At her feet lay a young boy about eleven years old. He lay face down in the rocks. His hair was matted with blood.

Pathki dropped to her knees. Gently she rolled the boy over. His face was streaked with blood. That wasn't what startled the girl. She couldn't believe her eyes. "This is Strong Runner. These are my people!" shouted Pathki. The girl's heart pounded with excitement. She had been led right to her people. They were the ones doing the deer surround.

Quickly Pathki swung into action. She unrolled her elkhide. She placed it alongside Strong Runner. With great care Pathki rolled the unconscious boy onto the hide. Grabbing her coyote hide, she rushed down to the nearby creek. She used it as a makeshift water bag.

Pathki returned with the precious water. She carefully washed the blood from Strong Runner's face. His cuts were not serious. Head wounds always bleed a lot. More serious than the cuts was the large bruise on the boy's forehead. It was already swollen badly. He had taken a very bad fall and would be in a coma for hours.

Pathki knew she could not leave him alone. When darkness came, wolves, bears, or mountain lions could find the helpless boy. "I have to hurry! I have to get help! Strong Runner could die here. I'll run to my people! I have to get help before darkness comes," the girl said to herself.

Before Pathki started her dash for help, she looked carefully at her surroundings. She must remember this exact spot. No time could be wasted looking for Strong Runner when she returned with help. Finally Pathki was sure she could return to this spot with no trouble. She took off, running for help. The frantic girl forgot about her own safety. She headed directly for her people. If she saw Cut Ears now, she would be running for her life, too.

Pathki ran only a short distance when suddenly she stopped in her tracks. What she saw ended her run right there. High above her on the northern ridge, Pathki saw a sight that sent a chill through her small body. Her plan to go for help would have to be postponed. On the rocks above, two huge mountain lions bounded from boulder to boulder as they crossed a large rock slide.

Do the two cats know about Strong Runner? she wondered. Had they caught the scent of fresh blood? Could Pathki hold them off until help came? The girl couldn't wait for answers. She knew she was needed back by Strong Runner's side. Her only thought now was to return to the helpless boy. Now he needed Pathki more than ever.

Quickly the girl retraced her steps to the fallen boy. She lost sight of the two lions. *Where can they be? How will I know when they're gone? When will someone come looking for Strong Runner?* The thoughts ran through Pathki's mind over and over. She knew she had only one choice. She must remain with the unconscious boy. Most important, she must find a way to keep the lions and any other dangerous animals from harming the boy, no matter how long it would take.

No one missed Strong Runner back at the village. Many deer had been killed. Everyone was busy cleaning the animals and hauling them to the village. No one was aware that Strong Runner had not returned. It would be dark before he was missed. Then it would be too late to begin a search.

Pathki realized that she, too, was in danger. When darkness came, it would be very hard to see approaching animals. It would be hard to beat back an attack. There wasn't enough time to start a fire. She needed to find another way to protect herself and her injured friend.

Pathki checked on Strong Runner. He was still breathing but very slowly. The girl had rolled him snugly into the elkhide. She looked all around her, knowing she had to do something fast. Pathki made her plan and went right to work.

As fast as possible, the girl began stacking rocks in a long line next to the boy. She used the largest rocks she could lift. She worked without even pausing to catch her breath. Two long walls on each side of Strong Runner began to take shape. When both walls were almost three feet high, Pathki filled in the narrow ends. Her rock fortress quickly took shape.

With the fortress walls complete, the girl hurried across the rocks to the trees. Pathki dragged two small dead trees to the fortress. She made several more trips to gather armfuls of dead branches. With these she fashioned a roof across the rock walls. Next she gathered a large pile of fist-sized rocks. Her plan was complete.

Pathki would stand guard all night. If the lions came, they would be met by a bombardment of rocks. They would hear all kinds of noises coming from the rock walls. The girl was ready when darkness came. The long night and the long wait began.

Pathki had lots of time to think. So much had happened to her in such a short time. It all seemed like a dream. Now the girl would have to wait out the long night. What would the next day bring? Should Pathki leave again in search of help? Would the boy she was trying to protect still be alive in the morning? Was there something else she could do to help him? These were big questions for a nine-year-old girl to worry about.

As the night wore on, Pathki's eyelids became heavy. Several times she dozed off for a few seconds. She fought to stay awake as a bright moon rose over the eastern mountains. The moonlight was so bright that Pathki could see shadows cast by nearby trees. The moon would help her keep a sharp lookout for danger. She spent almost all her time standing up at one end of the shelter.

The hours wore on very slowly. It seemed as if daylight would never come. Just when Pathki thought the mountain lions were not coming, she noticed a shadowy movement near the trees. She strained her eyes to see what it was. She could just barely make out the form of a crouching lion. In an instant Pathki sent a rock flying toward the lion. The missile slammed into a tree and bounced into the forest. The startled cat sprang forward and onto a large boulder. Pathki fired another rock. It ricocheted off the boulder just below the lion's paws. The big cat went bounding into the trees.

Pathki launched five more rocks into the trees. Next she started banging two rocks together. She began shouting at the top of her lungs. After five minutes of shouting and banging her rocks together, Pathki stood in utter silence. Her eyes remained fixed on the spot where the cat had disappeared into the trees. Minute by minute the girl grew more relaxed. The night dragged on and on. The lion did not return.

As the songbirds greeted the faint light of dawn, a weary Pathki dozed off. This time she was awakened by a coughing sound. It was coming from the elkhide. Strong Runner was coming out of his temporary coma. Quickly Pathki bathed the boy's head and face with clear cool water. She raised his head, propped it with the coyote hide, and held water to his lips in her cupped hands.

"Where am I? Who are you? What happened?" stammered Strong Runner.

The boy was suffering from temporary amnesia. He did not recognize Pathki. The girl tried over and over to get him to understand who she was. It was no use. Even as she talked to the boy, searchers from the village were on their way to find him. Pathki was still full of her fear of Cut Ears. She knew the searchers would come soon. *Will Cut Ears be with them?* she wondered. Could he be the first one here and find Pathki? Strong Runner would be of no help in his condition. The girl knew it was still dangerous for her as long as Cut Ears was around. Pathki decided to hide in the trees just above the fortress. She could keep an eye on the boy and give him help if it was needed. At the same time she would be hidden from the evil Cut Ears. Now another wait was beginning. This wait would be shorter and lead to more fear and more danger for the courageous girl to face alone.

10

Pursued Again

Pathki helped Strong Runner rise to a seated position. He was still unable to remember anything. He had no idea who Pathki was. The girl told Strong Runner to stay in the fortress until help came. The boy seemed to understand. Pathki made him comfortable, then left quickly.

The girl scrambled up the rock slide to a large boulder. From there she would be well hidden and still be able to see the fortress. She had to be sure that Cut Ears would not be the first one to find Strong Runner. If he was first, Pathki did not want to be found waiting there.

Pathki kept a close watch on the shelter. It seemed like a long time before the girl heard approaching searchers. She crouched down and anxiously waited to see the first people arrive. In minutes she hoped to be able to run down to her people and tell her story. Pathki was so excited the palms of her hands began to sweat. This was the moment she had awaited for a long time. She hoped her ordeal would be over soon.

The voices became louder and louder. Strong Runner heard them. The injured boy shouted for help. He hollered as loudly as he could. The searchers followed the sound of the boy's cries for help. When the two searchers came into view, Pathki's heart began pounding. Horror filled the girl's mind. She couldn't believe her eyes. There stood Cut Ears with a young boy. This boy was the person who saw Strong Runner last. Both boys had been together when the surround started.

Cut Ears tore the roof from the fortress and peered inside. There sat Strong Runner alive. Little Weasel jumped into the fortress to see how badly the other boy was hurt. When Little Weasel talked to Strong Runner, the injured boy just stared at him. Little Weasel knew his friend had hit his head very hard. The swelling had caused a large bump to form on Strong Runner's forehead.

Cut Ears looked at Strong Runner and didn't say a word. He fixed his eyes on the elkhide. He examined the rock fortress. He saw the coyote hide used as a pillow for the injured boy. Then Cut Ears started asking questions.

"Strong Runner, who helped you? Who made this shelter? Who gave you these hides?"

At first Strong Runner remained silent. He looked very confused. Cut Ears became impatient.

"Who helped you, boy? Where is this person now?"

"A girl helped me. I do not know her. I do not know where she is," stammered Strong Runner.

"Little Weasel, go for help! Strong Runner is sick. He needs help! Go! Go! I will find the person who helped him! Go!" urged Cut Ears.

Little Weasel headed off to find help. Cut Ears stood for a few minutes, scanning the ridges in every direction.

Pathki knew she was in great danger. Strong Runner couldn't tell Cut Ears her name, but he didn't have to. Cut Ears heard the word *girl*. That's all he had to know. He was sure Pathki was the one. He knew she was trying to get back to her people.

Pathki was already disappearing into the trees. She headed straight for the saddle on the ridge. It was the safest place to hide. From there she could see when it would be safe to run to her people. She still hoped to see her family that day. She was so close to success. She couldn't let Cut Ears find her first.

Little Weasel did not have to go far to find help. He led two men to the fortress. Soon other villagers arrived. Cut Ears was nowhere to be seen. When the people learned about Strong Runner's condition, they sent for a horse tied nearby. The weak boy was lifted onto the horse and all left for the village.

From her spot on the saddle, Pathki watched all this happen. She knew Strong Runner was safe. She had lost sight of Cut Ears. She had found a good hiding place with an excellent view of the valley. For now she felt safe.

Cut Ears was clever. He stayed hidden in the bushes and trees while he searched for signs of Pathki. He was quite sure the girl had come from behind the deer surround. Secretly and silently, Cut Ears made his way toward the saddle. The girl had no idea that danger was approaching one step at a time.

Pathki was well hidden in dense bushes. She blended in nicely with her surroundings. What caused the girl to come out of her bush for a better look, the girl could not explain. Something just made her feel uneasy. As she pushed the bushes apart to step out, she stopped, paralyzed by the scene just below her. There he was—only one hundred fifty yards away. The wind blew Cut Ears' hair away from his deformed ears. Luckily the evil one had stopped to catch his breath.

Terror gripped Pathki like a vise. *Hide! Where? There's no good place!* The terror-stricken girl scrambled on her hands and knees down the other side of the saddle. Far enough down so she couldn't be seen, Pathki jumped to her feet and dashed for the trees. She realized she was knocking down grass with each step. Cut Ears would be able to track her easily.

Pathki sprinted into the trees. Again she hid her trail by running on fallen trees. *Can this be?* she thought. *Is it all starting again? This can't be! I want to go home! I can't let Cut Ears catch me now.*

Cut Ears' stop to catch his breath had given Pathki just enough time for a short head start through the forest. She knew Cut Ears could travel fast. He could catch up in no time. Pathki was frantic. She had to find a hiding place—but where?

Just when the girl felt she would never find a place to hide, there it was. A large dead tree had fallen and landed against a live fir. The angle of this leaning tree made it a perfect ladder. It rested against the giant fir tree at a spot thirty feet above the ground.

Pathki headed straight for the base of the leaning tree. It was her only chance. She walked up the sloping log, steadying herself with her hands. In no time she disappeared into the branches of the great fir tree. Up she climbed. Just below the top, Pathki stopped, gasping for each breath. She draped her legs over two sturdy branches and hugged the tree trunk. Her breathing was loud and fast. She took some very deep breaths, knowing she had to get as quiet as possible before Cut Ears came close enough to hear her.

Cut Ears picked up Pathki's trail in the grass easily. He followed it to the trees. There the trail ended. Now he was sure this was the girl he was after. He asked himself, "Why had the girl left Strong Runner? What is she afraid of? She runs through trees as before."

Cut Ears had it all figured out. Now he was after Pathki again. The girl clung to the tree. Her breathing had returned to normal. She held herself taut. The hiding place she picked had better work. There would be no escape if Cut Ears spotted her in this tree.

The desperate man moved silently through the trees. He, too, walked the logs. He did it to avoid stepping on twigs and making noise. Cut Ears did not realize that a loose log lay directly in his path. As soon as he stepped on it, the loose log rubbed on the one next to it. A loud squeaking sound rang through the forest.

Cut Ears stopped. He looked in every direction. With his next step he came directly into Pathki's view. She couldn't see his face, only the top of his head. That was all she had to see. The man was directly beneath her.

There they were, the deformed ears. It was the evil one! It was the man who wanted to take her life. He was right below her.

Pathki's eyes never left this horrible scene. She held her breath. It seemed as if Cut Ears would never move away. *Why didn't he keep going? Can he feel my eyes watching him? If he sees me now, I will be caught. Why did I come up here? Has my guardian spirit left me?* Pathki clung to the tree petrified with fear.

The thirty seconds that Cut Ears stood below Pathki's feet seemed like thirty minutes. Finally he walked on. The girl closed her eyes. Her head rested against her life-saving tree.

Now Pathki had to plan her next move. She had plenty of time to think. She decided to stay in the tree until just before dark. Before it was too dark to see, she would carefully climb down. Once on the ground, she would wait until total darkness before returning to the fateful saddle of rock. From the saddle Pathki planned to walk the south ridge to her hiding place above the fortress. There she would spend the night. The next morning she would head along the top of the ridge toward her village.

The climb down was scary. On the ground the wait for darkness was short. Walking in pitch darkness was slow going. Pathki knew the moon would come up later. She had learned to read the moon and the stars as all Indian children did. Each night the moon rose later than the night before. Each night the moon's size changed a little. Pathki wanted to be in her hiding place before the moon appeared.

The girl arrived at her familiar hiding place above the rock fortress. Here she would spend another long night. She had no hide to sleep in. There were only rocks and hard ground. Pathki slept in short spurts. Every time she woke up, she looked and listened. The moon wasn't as bright as before. A few thin clouds filtered its light. Pathki knew the fortress lay just below, but she couldn't see it in the shadows.

Morning finally came. Pathki was weary and stiff. She had no food or water. She felt miserable. She didn't dare go near the creek. She didn't dare go anywhere in the open. Cut Ears could be watching. Maybe he, too, would return to the fortress. Pathki would not go near that place.

As the morning wore on, nothing stirred. The valley seemed completely deserted. Pathki began to relax a little. Her thoughts turned toward home. She could walk down the canyon to the place of the deer kill. From there she could follow her people's tracks to her village. She decided to wait and watch for a little longer and then head toward home.

Pathki kept looking at the sun. As the sun moved across the sky, it marked the passing of the day. The girl noticed the shadow cast by a sharp rock next to her. She decided to leave for her village when the shadow reached a large root. This was her solar stopwatch.

As Pathki moved around impatiently, she thought about her exciting arrival home. She planned to run right to her mother or Quiet One to warn them about Cut Ears. If she couldn't find them, she would have to find someone to believe her story and to protect her from the evil man.

Pathki turned to take one of her many checks of the shadow's progress toward the root. As she did, she heard a strange sound. Could it be? It sounded like someone laughing. Next Pathki heard voices. Someone was coming! Pathki dropped to her knees. She peered over her boulder. The opening around the rock fortress was quite large. Anxiously, the girl kept her eyes fixed on the scene below.

The voices grew louder. Then it happened. Pathki could not believe her eyes. Two young girls walked onto the rock slide and right up to the fortress. They stood with their backs to Pathki and looked into the fort. Pathki could not see who they were or make out their words.

Suddenly one girl turned and glanced straight up at Pathki's boulder. Pathki was shocked even more. *It's Red Willow! It's my sister!* Pathki was flooded with joy. Was it true? Was this a dream? The girl's heart was beating a mile a minute.

Pathki was ready to jump up and run down to Red Willow. To be on the safe side, Pathki quickly looked around for possible trouble. She didn't see any sign of Cut Ears.

The two girls had turned their backs to inspect the fortress once more. They didn't see Pathki stand up. Pathki was just about to shout Red Willow's name and run to her. In that split second Pathki swallowed her words. Her eyes caught sight of a moving shadow. Straight across from the fortress a shadow moved on the ground next to a large tree. Someone was hiding behind that tree! *Cut Ears!* she thought. *It must be Cut Ears! Who else would be hiding there?*

Pathki dropped behind her boulder and began shaking. Her thoughts sent chills through her small body. She told herself, "He is watching. I could have been seen. All of us would have been killed. Will I ever make it to my people? What should I do now? Oh! Guardian Spirit, help me! Help me!"

In the next few minutes the desperate girl would form a dangerous plan to make it to her village. She would not turn back now. She would take her chances against the vicious man who stood hidden behind a tree only a few hundred yards from her.

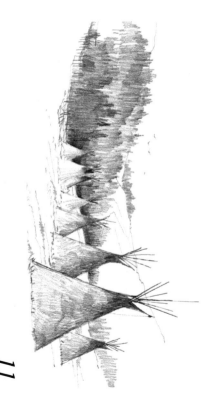

11

A Final Try

Pathki crouched behind the boulder. Her hands were shaking with the terror that poured over her. A mistake now could cost her her life. She moved to the left side of her boulder. Carefully Pathki peered around that side of the gigantic rock. Luckily a clump of chokecherry trees hugged that side of the boulder. The girl could look through their trunks without being seen.

Pathki saw Red Willow and the other girl sitting on the fortress wall. She could hear their voices but not clearly enough to understand them. Pathki fixed her eyes on the tree where she was sure Cut Ears stood hidden. The shadow was gone. Had Cut Ears left? Where was he now? Pathki had to know.

Pathki kept her eyes glued to the tree. She didn't have to wait long. There it was. The shadow was moving again. This time Pathki saw it even better than before. Then there *he* was. The man's head slowly moved into sight. There were the deformed ears again. It was Cut Ears. He was there, not one hundred yards from the fortress.

Pathki knew she was very fortunate to see the evil man before he saw her. The girl remembered hearing men tell stories of hunting adventures and dangerous battles with enemy warriors. In every story the men talked about how important it was to see your enemy before he saw you. In hunting, also, the men said that if the hunter could see the animal without that animal seeing him, the hunt would be much easier and more successful.

Pathki was so thankful that she had seen Cut Ears before he saw her. Now she would try to use this advantage to get back to her village safely. She saw Red Willow stand up and take one more look around. Then Red Willow said something to the other girl. The two girls stood next to each other for a few minutes more. Pathki watched them as they turned and headed back down the canyon.

Oh, how Pathki wished she could just walk back home with Red Willow, but she dared not move. Pathki kept her eyes on Cut Ears' tree. She would do her best to see what his next move would be. If she knew the direction he traveled, she could start making her plans.

Several long minutes passed without any movement by Cut Ears. Pathki took several deep breaths. At least Red Willow was out of danger for now. Still, it was hard for Pathki to stop trembling. In her own mind she knew she must try to return to her village. To go back to the wilderness would only delay the risk she would have to take sometime anyway. This was her chance. She would not let it slip by.

Pathki's eyes opened wide. Cut Ears was moving. She could see him walk right into the open. He was headed across the side hill and down the canyon. It looked like he planned to keep the two girls in sight. Pathki knew he would be hidden by trees most of the time. In fact, she lost sight of him right away.

Pathki decided to wait a few more minutes and then set her own plan into motion. She began by climbing higher on her ridge. She stayed well hidden and avoided making noise on loose rock or dead twigs. Near the top of the ridge Pathki turned left and started following the ridge down the canyon. She was on her way home!

The trip along the ridge was very slow. The side hill was steep. Loose rock had to be avoided. Grassy areas were slippery. In the trees downed timber made the going slow. The girl walked on and on, careful to remain well hidden.

Pathki soon came to a very dangerous place. It was a wide-open stretch of the ridge. She looked up and down the open area. She knew right away that it was an avalanche run. Every spring tons of snow roared down from the ridge crest above, wiping out everything in its path.

Pathki was terrified by this open area. Cut Ears could see her easily in the open. It stood like a barrier blocking her way. The girl had to think of something. She needed a safe way to cross this hazardous two hundred feet of open space. She thought about running. She thought about squirming through the grass on her stomach.

As Pathki stood surveying the scene, she looked across the valley. There were open areas there, too, where the side hill was steep. While the girl scanned the open places, she was distracted by a noise. It was falling rock. The sound grew louder. At first Pathki could not locate the cause of the sound. Then she saw dust rising from the opposite ridge. Rocks were tumbling down a rock slide and raising the dust.

Pathki's eyes traveled up the rock slide from the dust cloud. There he was! Cut Ears was just leaving the rock slide and disappearing into the trees. He had knocked a large rock loose. He had caused the small slide, more good luck for Pathki. Right at the most dangerous place on her ridge, she was able to see her enemy.

Pathki dropped to her hands and knees and scrambled across the open avalanche area. She was safely on her way again. Her guardian spirit was with her. She knew it. Pathki went on and on. She moved as silently as a mountain lion stalking a deer. Gradually the canyon narrowed. The girl was coming to a place where she would have to drop down very close to the trail. The ridge at the mouth of the canyon was nothing but sheer rock cliffs. This would be another place of great danger. Pathki did not want to meet Cut Ears on the trail. She was too close now for a deadly mistake.

Red Willow and her friend had already passed the narrows. They were walking past the place where many deer had been killed during the surround. Just ahead was a great surprise, not for the two girls but for Pathki. This surprise would finally end the girl's terror-filled ordeal forever.

Red Willow was almost to her village when Cut Ears passed her and her friend. He said he had been looking for a knife he had lost during the surround. He even asked if the girls had found it. He used these lies to cover up his real desire to find and kill Pathki.

Red Willow thought nothing about seeing Cut Ears out there. She was surprised to see another person on the trail just a few minutes later. It was her grandmother, Quiet One, walking very slowly up the trail toward her. The old woman said she was going out to be alone to talk with the Good Spirit. Red Willow knew her grandmother had been given great powers by the Spirit. Everyone in their village knew this. Red Willow just walked on.

Pathki slowly and silently moved down to the narrows. She was coming dangerously close to the trail. Now she moved from tree to tree and bush to bush. She kept well hidden. Her heart was pounding like a hammer when her eyes focused on the trail. She planned to inch her way by the cliff only twenty feet from the trail. As soon as she passed the narrows, she could go deeper into the trees and safely away from the trail.

Carefully Pathki moved ahead. The trail came closer and closer. Not twenty feet from the trail, Pathki froze in her tracks. There in the shadows next to the trail, Pathki saw a figure sitting on a log. She stood petrified in her tracks. She wasn't fifty feet from this person. The least little noise she made would be heard easily.

Who was it? Why was this person sitting there? Red Willow must have gone right past this one. Could it be Cut Ears?

Pathki's eyes had just begun to adjust to the dark shadows when the figure moved. The person rose to a standing position. Now this person moved forward. Never before had Pathki seen a more wonderful sight. It was Quiet One!

"Quiet One!" whispered Pathki. "You came! Thank you! Thank you!"

The girl leaped over the trees as she bounded toward her grandmother. The old one was startled by the excited girl. When Quiet One saw Pathki, she opened her arms. The young girl ran to the dear old woman. They threw their arms around each other. Tears streamed down Pathki's face. Her throat was choked up with her deep sobs of joy and relief.

Neither one said a word for several minutes. Finally Quiet One spoke. "Everything is all right, my child. You are home. You are safe. We worried about you. Sit with me. We will talk."

Pathki sat closer than ever to this one she loved so much. It would be several minutes before the girl could say a word. With her arms around Pathki, Quiet One asked Pathki to tell her story. She wanted to know what caused the girl to stay away so long. She said that the whole village thought she was dead. She told her about Cut Ears' tale of seeing Pathki killed and carried away by a grizzly bear.

Finally, Pathki could speak. She started from the beginning. She told about going out to seek her guardian spirit. She told about Cut Ears selling the horse, chasing her, the bear saving her life, her injury and her illness, and every detail of her survival away from her people.

When the shaking girl finished, Quiet One spoke. "You were wise and brave, my child. Your guardian spirit was with you. The elk, the swans, and the otters were with you. Now I am here for you. I heard the story of Strong Runner and how someone helped him live through the night. I knew that was you. I knew you were afraid to come to us. I did not know why. The Spirit sent me out here for you today. Now all of our people must hear your story. Come, we will go home."

How strange it seemed to be walking on a trail, right out in the open. There would be no more hiding and no more fear. Pathki couldn't believe it was really happening. As they walked along, the girl listened to her grandmother's plan.

"We will go straight to our village," said Quiet One. I will take you to your lodge. Then I will go to Cut Ears. I will tell him I know everything he has done. I will tell him he has only a short time to leave our village and the land of the Kootenai people forever. I will tell him our warriors will be ready if he ever returns."

Pathki was relieved to have Quiet One make the final plan to end her troubles. She walked very close to her beloved grandmother. The old woman circled the village and entered it near Two Birds' lodge. Pathki slipped into the lodge completely unnoticed. Quiet One left right away to find Cut Ears.

Pathki's wait was surprisingly short. Quiet One had found Cut Ears quickly. Cut Ears had a shocked look on his face as the old woman told him all she knew. He turned and left the village as fast as he could and never looked back. Pathki had won.

The news of the girl's return spread like wildfire. Everyone came to see Pathki for themselves. Children shouted her name. Never before had Pathki received so much attention. Before, the only attention she was used to was the bad kind she received when she had done something wrong.

Quiet One told the elders all about Cut Ears. Now they knew why he said Pathki had been killed. It all made sense now. The elders wanted to hear Pathki's story from her own lips. They had many questions.

It was a long story. Pathki did not leave out a single detail. The elders and all the people listened carefully. Every eye was on this nine-year-old girl. The more Pathki spoke, the more she was able to relax. It was as if a great burden was being lifted from her.

Pathki's story was the most unusual story these Kootenai people had ever heard a young girl tell. When she told about the otter family and the fish trapped in the willow branches, the elders had many, many questions.

As the girl finished her story, the elders knew this child had been taken care of by a powerful guardian spirit. Any time animals helped a human, it was a sign of good medicine. This girl had been helped by many animals, so the people knew she was a very special girl in the eyes of the Spirit.

The tribe's fishing chief talked to Pathki for a long time. He wanted to know all about the otters, the willow bush, and the fish. He asked Pathki if she could lead him to the place where the otters fished. He was anxious to see for himself. Pathki told him she could lead him right to the spot.

And so it happened—the girl who was always doing the wrong thing became the one who had saved a young boy's life. She became the girl whom the otters led to discover a new way to trap fish. She had been given the mighty elk. The trumpeter swan gave her the gift of the coyote hide. The Spirit had protected her from an evil man.

From that day on, Pathki would no longer be "the sad one." Suddenly she had become a young woman. From that day on, every member of this Kootenai village would respect Pathki Nana as a special member of their small band. They knew that like her grandmother she possessed special spiritual powers.

12

Soaring with Eagles

Now every day Pathki spent precious time with Quiet One. The young girl gained much wisdom and understanding from her loving grandmother. The wise old woman shared her years of living with young Pathki.

Pathki was saddened one day to hear Quiet One say that she would soon leave her granddaughter. The frail old woman said she would soon be leaving the earth for the spirit world. "When I die, my child, do not be sad. My life has been long. My joys have been many. When I die, my spirit will soar with the eagles to the land of the

159

Good Spirit. Be happy, my child. We have shared much with each other."

The day Quiet One died, Pathki was eleven years old. The girl sat at her grandmother's bedside, holding her hand. Quiet One's last words to Pathki would be carried in her heart and mind forever. "My child, your mother loved you so much. Two Birds loves you. I, too, love my granddaughter. Now you can take our love, put it in your heart, and share it with your children. Good-bye, my child."

With those words spoken so softly, Quiet One smiled at Pathki Nana, closed her eyes, took one last breath, and went to sleep forever. Pathki sat in utter silence. Tears streamed down her cheeks. The girl knew she had lost the one she loved the most on this earth.

Pathki put Quiet One's limp hand on her bed. The girl stood to leave. She felt weak and dizzy. Tears blurred her vision. Slowly the girl walked to the door of the lodge and went outside. The bright sun made it hard for the girl to see.

As Pathki rubbed her eyes, the girl heard a familiar screeching sound. It was the same sound she had heard while watching Cut Ears on the trail with the horse. Pathki shaded her eyes and looked into the bright blue sky. There they were. Two great bald eagles circled high above the village. Suddenly one majestic eagle screeched again and began a dive. The great bird swooped down straight for the village. Pathki was startled at first. Then she watched the powerful wings level off. The spectacular bird circled just above Quiet One's lodge. The white tail and white head shone brightly against the blue of the sky and the dark green of the fir trees.

After three very low passes over Pathki's head, the mighty eagle powered its way upward. The small girl watched as both marvelous creatures soared heavenward.

A smile came to Pathki's face. Quiet One's words were so clear that the girl thought her grandmother was with her again. "When I die, my spirit will soar with the eagles to the land of the Good Spirit."

Pathki stood smiling and waving to the soaring eagles.

"Good-bye, grandmother. Good-bye. I love you."

Quiet One's words and wisdom did live on in Pathki Nana for the rest of her life. Not a single day passed without this young girl remembering the words of the one she loved so much.